The Legend of the
Inn at Maiden Falls...

There are lots of rumors, but no one is exactly sure why even the crankiest twosomes get so very coosome when they spend time at the historic Inn at Maiden Falls, nestled in the Colorado Rockies. Maybe it's the beautiful vista of all that rushing water (the falls) outside the windows. Maybe it's the clean, invigorating mountain air stirring up their blood. Or maybe (as the whispers say) there really are lusty ghosts of shady ladies past floating around the rafters. Old-timers say the inn was a famous brothel more than a hundred years ago; all the "soiled doves" may have mysteriously passed away, but their spirits remain to help young lovers discover the joy of sensual pleasure. Or so the story goes....

Dear Reader,

Ghost hookers who haunt a honeymoon hotel where they spice up couples' sex lives? That's the idea Julie Kistler, Heather MacAllister and I brainstormed in July 2002 at the national Romance Writers of America conference in Denver, Colorado. And now, June 2004, our stories have come to life as my book, *Sweet Talkin' Guy*, kicks off our THE SPIRITS ARE WILLING Harlequin Temptation series!

In *Sweet Talkin' Guy*, heiress and runaway-almost-bride Daphne Remington crosses paths with Andy Branigan, a cynical reporter. He smells a hot story, she needs a place to hide out and they end up sharing one of the bridal suites while pretending to be newlyweds. What they don't know is their room is haunted by the once-notorious cardsharp and sharpshooter Belle Bulette, who thinks Andy and Daphne are hardly strangers but soul mates, and uses her ghostly wiles to prove as much.

To read about my upcoming books, check out my Web site at http://www.colleencollins.net.

Happy reading!

Colleen Collins

Books by Colleen Collins

COLLEEN COLLINS

SWEET TALKIN' GUY

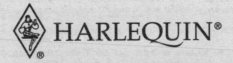

TORONTO • NEW YORK • LONDON
AMSTERDAM • PARIS • SYDNEY • HAMBURG
STOCKHOLM • ATHENS • TOKYO • MILAN • MADRID
PRAGUE • WARSAW • BUDAPEST • AUCKLAND

To Julie and Heather, with whom I had a ball brainstorming our ghostly world filled with divine hookers.

And to my editor, Wanda Ottewell, for her encouragement and insights, and for keeping me on course.

ISBN 0-373-69177-7

SWEET TALKIN' GUY

Copyright © 2004 by Colleen Collins.

www.eHarlequin.com

Printed in U.S.A.

The Golden Rules for
Miss Arlotta's Girls

We know rules are not your favorite things,
but some things need to be written down.
So here's your Golden Rules, girls. Abide by 'em
and we'll all do just fine. We weren't exactly angels
when we were here the first time around,
but we've got another chance. So we want to do what
we can to keep the idea of holy matrimony satisfying
so's nobody's man will be tempted to go lookin'
elsewhere for a good time. It may not seem fair,
but them's the rules. We helped 'em stray.
Now we're helping 'em stay.

Rule #1: You will never, ever do anything that might
come between the bride and groom.

Rule #2: No visibility. You can't be scarin'
the livin' daylights out of folks by fading in
and out or showing up in bits and pieces
at the wrong time.

Rule #3: Never, ever make love
with a guest yourself.
No exceptions.

Rule #4: No emotional attachments to
anyone. You can't follow them when they
leave, so you might as well not get attached.

Rule #5: When you have successfully put a troubled couple on the road to bedroom bliss, you earn a Notch in Miss Arlotta's Bedpost Book.

Rule #6: Especially good or bad activities may earn you Gold Stars or Black Marks.

Rule #7: It's gonna take ten Notches before you can advance. All Advancements shall be determined by Miss Arlotta and the Council, who will consider how difficult your couples were, how much work you had to do, your level of creativity, whether your heart was in the right place and those Gold Stars or Black Marks.

Rule #8: Any girl who disobeys these rules shall be punished.

Rule #9: Any and all rules may be changed by Miss Arlotta as she sees fit.

That's it. Push those couples into as much wedded bliss as they can handle, and we'll all do fine. You're all creative ladies when it comes to what happens between the sheets. So let's get to work and show 'em what kinds of sparks can fly when the spirits are willing!

Prologue

BEING DEAD isn't all it's cracked up to be. Good thing I died with my cigarillo clinging to my lip, a flask of whiskey in one hand and my trusty .44 in the other. Otherwise I'd be plumb out of luck for entertainment.

Belle Bulette pointed her Colt .44 at the god-awfulest, ugliest ceiling light she'd seen in at *least* a hundred years and cocked the hammer.

Across the parlor, the same room where over a century ago she and the girls had greeted their customers, Rosebud flashed a disapproving look through her wire-frame glasses before returning to her book, *Lady Chatterley's Lover*. The rest of the ghostly strumpets either made a great show of ignoring Belle or voiced their opinions of her.

"There she goes again, using the parlor for target practice," sniffed Flo, tossing a shawl over her nightgown.

Belle barely glanced in Flo's direction. The hooker's persnickety attitude had irked Belle in life and just did more of the same afterward. Whoever coined the phrase *rest in peace* had a thing or two to learn. Shame Mimi forgot to help Flo out of her too-tight corset the night of the fatal gas leak—otherwise, the ol' biddy might've spent eternity in a better mood.

"She was *much* better behaved when we were alive," chimed in Glory—oh, the men had once loved to shout "Glory, Hallelujah!"—in her thick Texas drawl.

"Balderdash," said Flo.

"She didn't shoot in the parlor," said Sunshine sweetly, her golden-blond hair as bright as the April late-morning rays pouring through the bay windows. "Or in any other room in the bordello. Well, although she *almost* did that time that varmint Blackhearted Jack got surly with Miss Arlotta and Belle told him to leave, her gun barrel wedged in his gut."

Belle wasn't much of a girly type—she'd always preferred the company of men—but she had a soft spot for Sunshine, who was one of her staunchest supporters. Plus, Belle had learned long ago that beneath Sunshine's doll-like looks was one savvy lady who knew *exactly* what she was doing.

Flo harrumphed. "Maybe Belle didn't shoot her gun in the house, but she sure rode that horse of hers into the foyer after too much red-eye. Miss Arlotta fined her a half eagle for *that* escapade."

"As though zat stopped her," murmured the Countess, as the Hungarian beauty primped in a mirror, her reflection seen by the girls but not by the living eye. "Belle never cared about za money."

Because I made enough to stock a woodpile. Belle still took great pride that right up until her and the girls' untimely death due to that nasty gas leak in 1895, she'd earned her living—and a handsome one at that—with her body *and* her mind. She'd plied her craft in the bedroom and at the betting table, saving most of her earnings so that one day she could open her own gambling house. When it came to cards, she was accustomed to winning, and when she won big, she celebrated big, too. Anyone could *walk* into a room and announce their good news, but it took balls to *ride* in.

Smiling at the memory, Belle lowered her pistol and took a drag of her cigarillo before again lining up the barrel with the ceiling globe. Hearing another of Flo's irritated harrumphs was almost as satisfying as the pungent taste of tobacco.

As if Belle could do any real damage. If her gun could shoot live bullets, that god-awful contraption would have been blasted away years ago. Bad enough their gas lamps had long ago been replaced with electrical lights, but that high-falutin' investment company who'd renovated their bordello into this fancy honeymoon hotel had darn near sucked the life out of it—painted over gold relief, ripped out oak paneling. Oh, they kept a few "touches of the past" in the lobby—the jewel-toned rug, mahogany fireplace, even added a few potted palms just like the girls had enjoyed many years ago. But the owners had relegated dang near everything else—*antiques* they called them—to an area in the back of the lobby set off with a red velvet rope and called the "historical parlor."

This parlor had once been what Miss Arlotta called the "high-rollers" room—nothin' *historical* about it—

where a gentleman could drink the finest whiskey and gamble for high stakes. It had been an honor for a girl to be summoned there and she often left by means of the secret staircase to the upper floors to keep her rendezvous discreet. If problems arose and a gentleman had to leave quickly, the staircase also had an exit to the side street.

On a few occasions, when no living people were around, Belle had materialized in this parlor so she could touch the faded red velvet chaise lounge or finger the delicate lace curtains. The room was crowded with memories of what it had been like to be alive and her mind would drift back to earthly delights. The brisk spray of water from nearby Maiden Falls during summer, the rush of wind in her face when riding her bay across the fields.

It'd been hell being housebound since 1895.

"Belle," boomed Miss Arlotta's voice. "No cussing."

Flo shot a supercilious look at Belle.

"Pardon," Belle murmured, glancing up at the attic where Miss Arlotta bided most of her time. Belle still hadn't figured out how the madam seemed to see and hear everything in this house, but she did. And when she spoke, her words reverberated through the air, commanding respect just as they had back when this was the classiest, fanciest bordello within a hundred miles of Denver.

And just as the girls had adhered to Miss Arlotta's rules back then, they abided by the madam's golden rules now, too. Of course, the focus had changed. As Miss Arlotta often reminded them, "Before, we helped 'em stray, now we're helping 'em stay." Married, that is.

Because when a girl helped a troubled couple on the road to bedroom bliss, she could earn a notch in Miss Arlotta's Bedpost Book. It was a coup to earn a notch first, because not all couples needed help. Second, because sometimes it took darn hard work to help the troubled ones—in special cases, Miss Arlotta rewarded bonus gold stars, worth more than one notch! Ten notches and a girl was eligible to advance to "the Big Picnic in the Sky."

Since the renovated Inn at Maiden Falls had opened in 1994—the first time the girls had had the opportunity to aid true love in compensation for the "fake" love they'd made in their earthly lives—Belle had earned nine. She was chomping at the bit to earn that last big notch, not caring if she advanced to the Big Picnic or the big cow pasture in the sky, just get her the hell—she darted a glance at the attic—the Sam Hill out of here so her spirit could once again be free.

"Will you look yonder?" said one of the girls. "Looks like we have a single gent checking into the inn."

"Just like in them grand old days," Glory chortled.

Single?

Belle swerved her gaze to the registration desk. Looking through the vapory form of Sunshine, who was chatting animatedly with another ghostly gal,

Belle checked out the tall, lanky man with the head of wild red hair. Didn't look like your typical just-married type. Dressed in blue jeans and a red fleece pullover with holes at the elbows, he looked more like a ruffian.

Some of the girls floated closer to the desk, commenting on his sporty appearance, lack of a wedding ring, those killer blue eyes. Living ones didn't hear the girls' chatter unless one materialized to them—which was a difficult feat and risked a black mark in Miss Arlotta's Bedpost Book. But once a couple had checked in to, and crossed the threshold of, a girl's room, she could materialize and speak to them as long as her goal was to spice up their sex life.

The ruffian leaned against the registration desk and Belle marveled at his long, lean legs. Men certainly didn't wear such muscle-revealin' jeans in her day.

"*Denver Post* reserved me a room six months ago," he said to the clerk.

The deep vibrations of his voice rippled through Belle. He had the kind of rock-bottom voice—low, gravelly—that reminded her of someone. But that'd been a long, long time ago.

"Oh yes!" said the desk clerk, a young girl who'd only been on the job a few weeks. "We've been expecting the *Post* and we're honored to be part of next month's feature on five-star honeymoon hotels in the Colorado Rockies and if there's anything you need or if we can be of any help..."

Yappity yap.

Belle had never been one for women's chitchat. Not during the thirty-two years she was alive nor the hundred and nine she'd been dead. She turned away and was wiping the pearl handle of her gun against her silk drawers when Sunshine floated up to her.

"That single gentleman is staying in *your* room, Belle," she whispered.

What?

Belle quickly floated to the desk and hovered over the computer monitor while gazing at the listing of rooms and names. Because of Belle's exceptional money-earning skills, Miss Arlotta had dedicated one of the rooms to her, the only girl to receive such an honor. The hotel, having unearthed this fact in their historical research, had named it Belle's Room.

She gasped.

Andrew Branigan, *Denver Post.* Belle's Room.

"Hellfire and—" She glanced up at the attic. "Pardon *again,*" she murmured, "but how in tarnation am I supposed to earn my last notch if I'm strapped with a single ruff—gentleman?"

Several of the ghostly gals giggled.

Belle shot them a withering look. Except for Rosebud, whose rip-roarin' smarts had always set her apart, they all stared back looking a tad frightened.

Dang, darn and pshaw!

Taking her old shootin' stance, Belle straightened her arm and pointed the .44 at the ugly globe. Ignoring the girls' squeals and threats, she squeezed the trigger. The shot tore loose with a crack and flash, only witnessed on their ghostly realm. The bullet, as always, disappeared into nothingness.

Or into another world.

The world where, Belle believed, she'd someday be. And yearned to go. But with a single guy in her room... Well, hell's bells, she might as well twiddle her thumbs because she wasn't goin' nowhere soon.

"Belle, no—"

"Yes, Miss Arlotta, no cussing. No Big Picnic in the Sky, either." She tucked her gun in the waistband of her drawers and floated up the stairs, needing some breathing room...

As though *that* were possible. No breathing, no sex, no cussin'.

Being dead isn't all it's cranked up to be.

1

DAPHNE REMINGTON, socialite and bride-to-be, chewed thoughtfully on a strip of raspberry licorice as she scrutinized herself in the full-length dressing-room mirror. "Why do brides have to wear white?" she murmured. "I look so much better in red."

"It isn't white, it's ivory," countered the salesclerk as she adjusted one of the dress straps. She lowered her voice conspiratorially. "Besides, after that stunt you pulled several years ago at the Firecracker Ball, I figured you'd never wear red again."

Over the past few months of Daphne trying on the latest bridal designs at Ever-After, the ultra-exclusive salon in the ultra-exclusive Cherry Creek area of Denver, she and the salesclerk, Cindi, had become chummy enough to drop the me-sales person, you-client facade. Plus, not only were they both pushing thirty and feeling familial pressure to marry, they both confessed to serious bad-boy fantasies about the wild Irish actor Colin Farrell—and if *that* didn't bond two women, Daphne wasn't sure what else could.

"Well, I don't wear red in *public* anymore, especially around swimming pools," Daphne said with a wink, which made Cindi laugh.

That was because everyone who had read the *Denver Post* three years ago on July fifth had seen a picture of socialite Daphne Remington being hauled out of the Denver Country Club pool, her red silk dress clinging to every inch of her body. The *Post* had labeled the photo Renegade Remington which had been bad enough to live down, but then the story got picked up by the AP wire and had ended up in papers and magazines across the country with captions like Red-Hot Remington! and Haughty Hot Heiress. *Playboy* had even approached her to do a special photo shoot.

Her family had not been amused.

Not even when she tried to explain that she'd jumped in on a dare—a handful of guys had collected several thousand dollars, betting she wouldn't jump into the pool fully clothed. Loving a challenge—and emboldened by several flutes of champagne—she'd kicked off her Manolos and executed a flawless jack-knife.

But did the papers snap a picture of that moment of stylistic perfection? No-o-o. They'd gone for the grossly unflattering shot of her soaked head to toe, her hair matted and tangled, with mascara smeared underneath her eyes like some kind of prizefighter.

The following morning, when Daphne stumbled to the breakfast table to find the front page of the *Post* on her chair, she'd explained to her parents that despite appearances, she'd *personally* raised more money at the fundraiser than any other single contributor.

They continued not to be amused.

Which was par for the course. Delores and Harold Remington III, icons of Denver society, had never been pleased with their eldest daughter's rebellious nature. And as she'd done mega times before, Daphne listened to their lectures about how her great-great-great-great-grandfather Charles "Charlie" Remington had only a quarter in his pocket when he'd staked his mining claim in the Colorado Rockies. How, through hard work and perseverance, he'd not only struck gold but segued his fortune into a real-estate empire. How his offspring were politicians, doctors, lawyers who'd fought for justice and left the world a better place. How her only sibling, the ever-reputable and perfect Iris, was following the path of outstanding, law-abiding Remingtons...

Left unspoken was that rebellious Daphne had still to find the path. Daphne bet even Paris Hilton's parents gave her more consideration than Daphne's own did her.

Nevertheless, after the infamous Firecracker Ball incident, Daphne had done her best to behave. No wild escapades, no outrageous clothes. It was like being in a twelve-step program for bad girls, but she'd done it because she truly didn't like embarrassing her family. Of course, having her parents threaten to withhold her trust—a cool two and a half mil that was hers on her wedding day—unless she "shaped up" was an incentive.

During that period, her parents had introduced her to G. D. McCormick, a prominent lawyer who was eight years older, sophisticated, with a stellar career as a partner at the prestigious Denver law firm Joffe, Marshall and McCormick. Daphne hadn't liked him for those attributes, however. He'd had a kick-back side that was fun, lighthearted. Plus, he professed to love her "high spirits."

When, after dating for a year, he'd asked her to marry him she'd said yes. Maybe she didn't feel that zap of lightning Mario Puzo wrote about in *The Godfather*, but that was fiction after all and she was in the real world. Her family was thrilled, her friends were giddy and Daphne was happy and relieved that finally she was on *the path*.

But the happiness had taken a downward turn six months ago when the state's top-dog politicos had asked G.D. to be their candidate for governor next year. That's when G.D. became less kick-back and more kick-ass. Increasingly concerned with his political image, his adoration of her high spirits became criticism of her free spirits. If she'd had a quarter for every time he'd asked her to tone down her wardrobe or her language, she probably could have paid off half the city of Denver's current budget deficit.

G.D. had even started criticizing her way of walking. Seemed her hips swung too far left and right when she walked. She quipped that she'd swing the way of his political leanings, but he—like her family— wasn't amused.

Daphne's high spirits were low ones more and more.

She looked in Ever-After's dressing-room mirror and fluffed her normally straight dark hair, which was resorting to its natural curl thanks to this morning's April showers. "When we first dated, G.D. and I used to have spontaneous adventures," she suddenly said. "We'd grab cheese and bread for a picnic or hop a bus and visit some picturesque spot in Colorado. I'd take my camera and snap photos..." Her voice trailed off.

Cindi, checking something on the hem, looked up. "Politicians can't afford to be spontaneous. Bad for their image."

Daphne nodded, taking another bite of licorice. Many nights she'd lain in bed, hoping G.D.—Gordo— would change his mind about running for office. Her life was enough of a fishbowl without being married to a governor.

"Oh, sweetie, don't look so sad. After the wedding, your lives will settle down. You'll get into campaigning, learn the ropes about being a politician's wife."

"That's what my mother keeps saying." Daphne sighed heavily. "But a governor's wife? *Me?*"

"My mom said Linda Ronstadt was almost a governor's wife when she dated Jerry Brown. If a rocker almost did it, shoot, it'll be a cinch for you."

"If you'd said Madonna, I'd feel better."

"Hey, she's written a children's book."

"Let's hope they don't mix it up with one of her other books during some kiddie story hour."

Cindi laughed.

"Seriously," continued Daphne, "I guess you're

saying there's hope for Renegade Remington." But even Daphne heard the lack of hope in her tone, which was starting to sound more like the voice of doom.

Cindi touched Daphne's arm. "Hey, sweetie, I have an idea. Want to try on some slinky lingerie? Something hot for your wedding night? We just got a shipment of sheer, strappy chemises that are to die for!"

Daphne began slipping out of the wedding dress. "Girlfriend," she said, forcing herself to sound exuberant, fun—not so long ago she never had to force that attitude—"bring them on!"

A few minutes later, Daphne had doffed her bra and was slipping into a bottle-green silk chemise with black lace trim that hovered seductively at the top of her thighs. "Cool," she purred, eyeing herself in the mirror.

"Some girls are wearing them with skirts and pants. It's the new skimpy-chic look."

"I couldn't wear it in Denver..."

"Take a trip out of town. Somewhere remote, where no one knows you."

Anonymity. What a treat it would be to be invisible, a face in the crowd. Nobody watching, judging...

Daphne put on her cargo pants and tucked in the chemise. She looked at her reflection. "The pièce de résistance," she said, stepping into the lime-green Prada heels that gave her bare calves a nice curve.

"You got *it*," Cindi murmured.

"I do, don't I?" It was fun to let down her guard, to be sassy and playful again. She turned sideways, admiring the effect. "I like dressing in different shades of the same color...some days it's pink, others all blue. Today felt like a green day."

"Because it's April?"

Daphne paused. "Maybe. Spring and new beginnings and all that."

From the other room, a phone trilled

Cindi stepped toward the door. "Gotta grab that. Hey, check out the turquoise lace camisole on the lingerie rack."

"Twist my arm," teased Daphne, following her out of the dressing room.

As Cindi chatted on the phone, Daphne fingered through the sheer, silky lingerie. Outside the tinted windows, she looked down on Denver's elegant Detroit Avenue.

Jaguars and Beemers cruised down the road. Across the street thin women sipped espressos at a sidewalk café, their groomed dogs sunning nearby. Baskets of bright spring flowers hung from lamp posts. Everything cultured and sophisticated and perfectly perfect...it was as though she were looking into a glass ball at her future life.

She shivered involuntarily, and had started to turn away when something caught her attention.

An old school bus, painted gray with gold trim, sputtered down the street. On its side in cursive script was painted Maiden Falls Tour Bus in bright red.

Maiden Falls. The former mining town in the Rockies, next to where, in the 1880s, her ancestor Charles had staked his claim, Last Chance. It was now a state-preserved historical site. But despite all his riches, for the rest of his life Charlie swore his happiest days were when he'd been a poor and struggling miner.

And could that have had anything to do with your being camped next to Maiden Falls? Daphne grinned, imagining her four-times-great-gramps, before he found the bride of his dreams, being pretty darn happy camped next to Maiden Falls—the tongue-in-cheek term for the ladies of the evening who'd set up business there. After years of usage, the name had stuck. Maiden Falls was now the official town name, a place filled with quaint shops and a lovely old renovated hotel.

At one time, she and Gordo would have been spontaneous and hopped on this Maiden Falls tour bus for a spur-of-the-moment adventure. He'd always justified these excursions with an old legal saying, "No consideration, no contract." But what he really meant was hey, if you really wanna do it, it's a deal.

Daphne's toes twitched as she yearned to break loose, to do something impulsive again.

The bus parked outside the café, next to a sandwich-board sign with Tours written in large black letters on it. A skinny kid in jeans and a baseball cap jumped off the bus and stood next to the Tours sign. Several people—who appeared to have been waiting at the café—began lining up, buying tickets.

Daphne watched, mesmerized, as, one by one, people purchased tickets and got on the bus.

The bus that would be leaving soon.

Her toes twitched again.

G.D. was out of town for the weekend at some po-litical rally. Her parents had back-to-back society functions over the next few days. And her perfectly perfect sister was too self-absorbed to really care what big sis Daphne did.

It's my last chance to be free, adventurous. Even Cindi said I should escape to some remote town, far away from the rules of high society. If someone asks, I could say I'm any-body, a location scout for a film, a grad student researching old mining towns…

Plus, just as ol' Charlie Remington had enjoyed his greatest happiness in those hills, maybe so would she. Simple, unadulterated, un-whispered-about-behind-her-back happiness.

That cinched it.

Grinning, she rushed back into the dressing room, tossed on her jean jacket and grabbed her purse. Run-ning through the salon while buttoning up the jacket, she pointed to the top of her chemise and mouthed "Put it on my bill."

Cindi nodded, her eyes growing wide as she contin-ued talking on the phone.

Half jogging across the street, Daphne felt the ex-quisite flutterings of an impending grand escape—the way she used to feel all the time. Damn, it felt great to be alive again! Alive and free-spirited, escaping the uptight, rule-oriented world of Cherry Creek.

As she slipped into line for the tour bus, she pulled out her wallet. Fifty dollars cash and a handful of credit cards. Plenty of ammunition for anything she might need on this trip.

As Daphne paid the lanky kid twenty-five dollars for the round-trip ticket, he said, "Have a wonderful trip, ma'am, to Maiden Falls."

Ma'am? She grinned as she stepped onto the bus. Screw the location scout or grad student fantasies. For these next few days, she'd be a *maiden*—a fallen maiden—enjoying her last adventure in Maiden Falls!

ANDY BRANIGAN sat in a small parlor nestled in the back of the lobby at the inn at Maiden Falls staring at the sepia-toned photo in the old album, wondering if Maiden Falls was named for this particular group of fallen maidens...or any of the other ladies of the evening who had flocked to Colorado's mining towns back in the late nineteenth century.

Looking at this picture, however, one would be hard-pressed to claim these were shady ladies. This group was dressed in their Sunday finest, sitting demurely on a blanket in a field having a picnic. Some held parasols, some daintily nibbled on fried chicken.

One would never guess this was a group of hookers who had plied their wares in this very honeymoon hotel, the same place where a savvy Madam Arlotta had once managed her lucrative business and the working girls.

Honeymoon hotel? More like a bridal bordello.

Hmmm, not bad.

He pulled a small spiral-bound pad out of his shirt

pocket and jotted down *bridal bordello*. He stared at the words, hearing Frank, his boss and the *Denver Post*'s features editor, bellowing, "Forget it, Andy. You're a sweet-talkin' guy with a way with words, but no way in hell we're printing a piece on *honeymoon* hotels titled Bridal Frickin' Bordello."

Andy tucked the notepad back into his pocket, behind his pack of cigarettes, planning his rebuttal. "Frank, buddy, if you wanted safe and sensible, you shouldn't have sent your best reporter out to write this fluff piece."

Frank would start to argue.

That's when Andy would nod, as though commiserating with Frank's stance, but then he'd say, "Hey, paper's circulation's down. You need to boost readership. I'll write lace and nicety for other honeymoon spots, which women will eat up. But keep the bridal-bordello angle for this place and you'll woo the male readership, too. Win-win, Frank."

Andy stared at the No Smoking sign, debating whether to sneak a cig here or step outside. He was toying with testing where a door in the back of the parlor led when a maid opened it. She smiled at him before starting to dust the parlor. That explained the door—had to be some kind of housekeeping stairwell.

He'd head out through the lobby, catch a smoke on the porch outside.

He started to close the album, when a figure at the back of the picnic photo caught his eye.

One of the ladies held a gun, lining up a shot. She

was dressed prettily, just like the others, but that dead-eye look she gave her target revealed this was no shrinking violet. And he'd seen that tumble of hair before in other historical photographs.

"Belle Bulette," he murmured, admiring her strong profile, her spread-legged stance.

One of the soiled doves he'd researched before arriving at this hotel yesterday. He'd requested the Bulette Room, named after this working girl who he'd figured had traveled to Maiden Falls around 1890, maybe '91, to ply her trade with the growing number of miners in the area. But Belle had had other tricks up her sleeve, like a wicked skill with cards.

And although the history books hadn't made the link, he felt strongly the name *Belle* was made up, a label she'd picked after arriving in Maiden Falls to protect a dark incident in her past.

Such facts Andy had compiled from his extensive research on ghost towns and mining towns in the southwest. A love of history that had started back when he was a kid growing up not far from here, privy to the stories his grandfather—the man who'd raised him—and his cronies had told and retold about what their fathers and grandfathers had said about the wild, wild west.

He closed the book and returned it to a side table, then looked around at the lush Victorian decor of this "historical parlor"—as it was advertised on the plaque outside the room. According to the inscription, this room was a replication of how the bordello's main parlor, now the lobby, had looked back in the 1890s, the place where the ladies had met their customers before taking them upstairs. This historical parlor was filled with everything from photo albums and other memorabilia to an impressive white marble mantelpiece and so much red velvet, the room was like a frickin' bleeding heart.

Made him claustrophobic.

He headed out of the room into the stylishly decorated and light-filled lobby and grabbed several cookies off a sideboard. A couple lolled on the nearby couch, the young woman hand-feeding a cookie to the man who was nibbling more at her fingers than the confection.

Andy gave himself a mental shake. No woman would ever hand-feed *cookies* to Andy Branigan. If she did, it sure as hell wouldn't be in a *honeymoon hotel.*

As Andy chewed, a sweet scent, like lilacs, wafted past. A lady's perfume. He looked around, but no one else had entered the parlor. Odd.

Oh, he'd heard the stories about how this place was haunted by shady ladies of the past, but he didn't believe such nonsense. Ghosts were about as real as true love. Both were fabrications of minds that needed a better grip on reality.

A woman's voice caught his attention.

"What do you mean no rooms? I'll pay double, triple what anyone else is paying!"

Partially blocked by an oversize potted palm was the antique registration desk. If he craned his neck a bit, he caught the rump of a woman leaning over the desk, a pair of cargo pants ending mid-calf, her feet tucked into a pair of lime-green heels.

"The Inn at Maiden Falls is booked ahead for months," murmured the voice he recognized as the portly hotel manager. She'd intervened earlier after the young desk clerk had realized his room wasn't ready, wouldn't be for several hours. The manager had apologized, offered him a complimentary gift certificate to the inn's five-star restaurant, the Golden Rule, or one of the local restaurants.

He'd picked Pete's Pizza down the street.

"And the problem is?" said the female voice, tapping a high-heeled foot against the polished hardwood floor. "Surely someone would appreciate not only having a complete refund, but extra money for a side trip or maybe a honeymoon suite in a, uh, better located hotel."

"The inn is located in one of the most beautiful spots in the country—"

"I didn't mean *that*. I meant a hotel in the city, close to museums, shopping centers. A suite in Denver's Brown Palace, for example."

"Perhaps you and your husband should go to Denver, check into the Brown Palace."

"I just arrived from Denver! I want to stay *here!*"

Spoiled. Andy avoided those types like the plague. They always wanted guys to blow big bucks on them for dinners, theater, overpriced frothy cocktails. But rare to find a spoiled princess alone, desperate to pay

two or three times the already substantial price for
a room.

Andy had a nose for news stories, and this definitely smelled like an interesting one.

He knocked off the second cookie while ambling
closer. Leaning against a settee, he checked out the
woman.

Slim and toned. Pretty calves. Tight ass. He imagined her in one of those thong numbers, treading an
exercise machine, sweat trickling down her pink,
moist skin.

He shifted a little to ease the sudden tightness in his
groin.

He stared at her high-rise pants. He always appre-
ciated a flash of flesh, but it was still a bit cold in the
mountains to be wearing anything that exposed skin.
Plus snow from last week's storm still dotted the
ground—hardly the kind of terrain to navigate in
neon skyscrapers. Wearing heels in a mountain town
was like wearing flip-flops to climb Mount Everest.

She obviously hadn't planned for this trip.

She gestured as she spoke and he caught the pink
Rolex on her wrist. And on her ring finger, a diamond
that could double for a search light.

Engaged. Rolling in dough. Why run away to this
inn? Why not hop in her Jag—or Lexus or Mercedes—
and scoot down the highway to some private, exclu-
sive spa?

The manager explained there was a boarding house
in a neighboring town.

The princess almost-bride huffed and turned her head enough for Andy to catch her profile.

He stared at the impertinent nose, flashing hazel eyes, red-slicked lips. Reminded him of the young Katherine Hepburn. He wondered if just like the movie star, underneath this woman's steel spine smoldered a passionate heart...

Her eyes caught his.

Their gazes held for a moment before she looked away, returning to her discussion.

He'd seen this lady before....

The hair looked different—curlier—but she was definitely familiar. Andy quickly sifted through his memory, flipping through a catalog of images from his various assignments. No, she was too well dressed to be one of the contemporary cowgirls he'd recently written a piece on. And although her haughty air was similar to the ballerina he'd interviewed last year, she'd had a bit more meat on her.

No, he hadn't written or interviewed her, but he'd definitely seen her somewhere.

Bam!

"Renegade Remington," he said under his breath.

He crossed his arms over his chest and eyed the privileged daughter of one of Denver's bluest-of-the-blue-blood families. Their name was everywhere. The Remington Wing of the Children's Hospital. The Remington Theater Arts Complex. Even the recently christened Remington Avenue that ran adjacent to the Denver Country Club.

Ah, yes, the Denver Country Club and the scandalous photo of Daphne Remington. Andy flashed on the picture of her being tugged out of the pool, a crimson dress molded to a shapely body. Funny, she'd slipped below the radar after that...reemerging in tasteful society stories, often pictured on the arm of G. D. McCormick, high-profile lawyer and up-and-coming gubernatorial candidate.

Weren't they supposed to be getting married soon? That explained the boulder-sized ring.

Andy felt a tingling on the back of his neck—an electric warning that he'd stumbled on a hot lead. A runaway heiress story, a runaway almost-bride story...maybe both?

It smacked of that Julia Roberts surprise wedding escapade, one he and the guys at the paper wished they'd broken.

This was *that* kind of story. A "Runaway Renegade Remington" escapade. Not only was the family name known in Denver, but all over the country thanks to the parents' upper-crust jet-setting and their philanthropic donations.

This was the kind of hot scoop national magazines and television stations paid big bucks for. The kind of moola that could propel Andy out of being a reporter in the trenches and give him the means to research and write the book of his dreams—the definitive book on Colorado history he'd wanted to write since he was a kid.

Daphne was tapping her diamond-heavy hand on

the polished wood of the registration desk. "Well, I can't believe you'd turn down such a good deal."

"In the future, please make your reservation ahead of time and we'll happily accommodate you."

The woman didn't sound very happy at the prospect, however.

Daphne pivoted on those skyscraper heels and minced to the door, a leather purse slung over her jean-jacketed shoulder.

No luggage.

That cinched it. Daphne Remington had definitely traveled here on a whim.

Oh yes, baby, this was one hot scoop.

As the front door clicked shut behind her, Andy followed, thinking how Frank would beg for this story, but Andy would have already made some sweet deals elsewhere.

Hot scoop? Andy chuckled to himself. *More like molten.*

2

DAPHNE SAT on the red vinyl stool at the drugstore soda fountain. She stared forlornly out the window at the Inn at Maiden Falls across the street, admiring its pink-and-raspberry exterior.

I belong there. It even wears colors the way I do.

A blast of noise distracted her. She glanced at a compact TV on a shelf next to coffee cups and fountain glasses. On its screen, a baseball player wielded a bat, his jaw tight, his eyes focused. *I probably looked like that at the hotel, minus the bat.*

But despite her determination, Daphne had failed to get a room. There was a time when she could talk her way into anything. Once, in Vegas, she'd convinced a nightclub owner to let her *and* two girlfriends into a No Doubt show. What a night that had been. Fun, carefree, back before she'd worried about things like what the press might say if she did this or that.

When did I lose my touch? Or maybe I've lost my confidence?

Daphne popped open the top buttons on her jacket as she glanced at the inn again. It was hot as blazes in this drugstore.

An older gentleman sidled up behind the counter,

tufts of white hair sticking out underneath a Rockies cap. "Walker," he barked at the TV, "you're paid too much to strike out!" He looked back at Daphne. "What can I get ya?"

"Diet cola, slice of lemon. And—" she fanned herself "—could you turn down the heat?"

He rolled his eyes toward the kitchen. "The better half's always cranking it up. I'll turn it down."

"Thank you."

"Anything else?"

"Lime phosphate," answered a deep, gravelly male voice. "And an order of chili fries."

"Ya got it." The older man sauntered away.

Daphne looked over at the man who had settled on the seat next to her. Piercing blue eyes and a thick, unruly mass of rust-golden hair grown unconventionally long. She wondered if that don't-give-a-damn look was calculated or if he really didn't care about current styles.

Although...picking the seat right next to her was definitely calculated. Every other stool was empty.

"Couldn't find another seat?" she asked.

He looked down at hers, then back up. "The one I wanted was taken."

A rush of heat blasted through her. "You're impudent," she said, which would have sounded outraged if her voice hadn't gone all breathy. She was seriously out of practice with bad-boy come-ons.

"My apologies."

From the twinkle in his blue eyes, she didn't believe

he was sorry for a millisecond. Not trusting her traitorous voice, she gave a half nod as though accepting his apology.

He leaned forward and she caught a flash of tie-dyed shirt underneath a red fleece pullover. "Caught your give-me-a-room speech across the street."

He was watching? She glanced out the window again at the inn. If he'd been standing on the hotel porch, he could easily have seen through the windows into the lobby, but she doubted he'd heard any of the conversation between her and that obstinate desk clerk.

Although, on second thought, Daphne recalled briefly making eye contact with some man standing behind her. She'd been so irritated, however, she'd barely registered who he was.

But now she knew.

It was him.

Which meant he was staying there. At *her* hotel. The place where she desperately wanted to spend one last carefree, anonymous weekend.

Daphne looked past the man, searching the aisles of beauty items, and at the small pharmacy beyond for a newlywed Mrs. Impudent.

"I'm alone," he said, reading her searching gaze.

Daphne tucked a curl of her hair behind her ear. "That wasn't necessarily what I was thinking." *Like I'd admit it.* She cleared her throat. "But since you mentioned it, seems strange to stay alone at a honeymoon hotel."

"Strange?" He cocked a sardonic eyebrow, his eyes glistening. "No, sad. Very, *very* sad."

A feeling rippled between them. A sizzle of attraction that charged the air.

She became overly aware of his hand on the counter, how close it lay to hers. And she recalled something her great-aunt had once said—that a person's hands were either muscled like a worker's or long-fingered like an artist's. She didn't want to stare, but...

His were both.

"Here ya go!" said the older gentleman, jarring her out of the moment. He set the cola in front of Daphne and a glass filled with a slushy green concoction and a plate piled with a greasy mess in front of the guy. "Anything else I can do for ya?"

When they shook their heads no, he jabbed his thumb toward the TV where a television reporter spoke earnestly to the camera. "Want it off?"

Just then, a photo of Daphne flashed on the screen. Well, a photo of her standing in the background behind G.D., who, the reporter was explaining, had just won a major legal case involving corporate fraud. The story segued into G.D.'s possible bid for governor and his pet issues of tourism, reemployment assistance and promotion of Colorado's agricultural products.

She'd heard it all before, a hundred times, had even been coached on how to respond to those same topics herself. And damn if Gordo didn't wind up his legal

victory speech with the sound bite, "No consideration, no contract."

"Yes, turn it off," answered Daphne, not wanting to
hear more. Didn't want to be recognized, either, as the
woman in the background. But she doubted either
man had recognized her. In the photo, her hair was
pulled back in a tight chignon, the exact opposite of
the curly mass she wore today. And that god-awful
dress in the photo was one of those matronly ensem-
bles her mother had insisted she wear. Proper and all
that.

*Probably overreacting. Who would look at me in that
photo, anyway? The focus is on G.D.* Was it her imagination, or did she look smaller standing in the background? Definitely insignificant.

With a chilling realization, Daphne saw her future.
Small, insignificant, always in the background of
G.D.'s life.

Her insides contracted a little.

The older man flicked a knob and silence descended.
After sliding the bill across the Formica counter, he
ambled away.

Andy shoved the plate of goop steaming with spice
and grease toward her. "Help yourself."

She wrinkled her nose. "What is it?"

"Fries topped with chili, chopped onions, jalapeños." With a pleased guttural sound, Andy dipped
his fingers into the mess. She wondered if he dove into
life like that, indulging himself the way an animal
gleefully rolls in the dirt just because it feels good.

"I'll pass."

"Shame—you're missing out on something good." He shoved chili-drenched fries into his mouth. After swallowing, he frowned. "Your perfume—" he nudged the air with his nose "—smells different than before."

"How can you possibly smell anything through that..." She glanced at the pile of grease, cheese and fries.

He took a silver flask out of his pants pocket, shooting her a wry smile. "When I first sat down I could've sworn I caught a whiff of roses and not lilacs."

"Lilacs?"

"The scent I caught back at the hotel."

He hadn't been standing close enough to pick up the scent of her perfume. And Daphne wasn't the type to splash the stuff on, especially not at several hundred dollars an ounce. "It's called Dulcinea." G.D. never commented on her perfume. Not anymore.

"Dulcinea," he murmured, rolling the word on his tongue. "The personification of Don Quixote's dream." He looked at her. "Don Quixote de La Mancha? Ever read the book?"

"I'm more a contemporary type." She recalled those antiquated literature assignments at the private school in England. Truly a hideous time in her life, cooped up, wearing those insane school uniforms that made her look like some kind of nun-in-training. Just as she'd finally discovered an escape route through a hole in the fence—ah, freedom—and the fields beyond where she'd run barefoot, she'd also discovered an escape route with her studies. Thank God for those little yellow pamphlets that offered abridged notes on ponderous literary tomes.

"Funny how people forget that writers were all 'contemporary types' in their time. Anyway, what's cool about Don Quixote is his ability to see others' hidden beauty, which he loves with unshakable faith. That love gives him the energy to enter into great battles, to accomplish noble deeds, to become a heroic knight."

The way he spoke, his words edged with reverence, took Daphne by surprise. With his worn clothes and cocky in-your-face attitude, he didn't seem like the kind of man to appreciate a romantic story of love and dreams. Even more astounding that he'd taken the time to wade through an old masterpiece, word by word.

"You have a love of words."

He tipped his flask, pouring liquid into his glass. "Yeah, they call me a sweet-talkin' guy."

For books *and* for the ladies, she'd bet. "That's alcohol," she said, eyeing his flask.

"Why, yes, I believe you're right." He picked up a knife and stirred his drink. "Vodka to be exact."

"I don't believe this establishment has a liquor license."

"Gonna turn me in?" He jiggled the flask at her before returning it to his pocket. "'Cause if you do, I might get tossed into jail. Which would make it rather difficult for you to share my room at the inn."

"Share—?" She made a derisive sound. "This is a soda fountain, not a singles' bar."

He slid a look to her neckline. "And from that flash of black lace and see-through silk, it's obvious you know the difference, too."

Heat flooded her cheeks. "You're—"

"Impudent. I know." He held her gaze and she felt another wave of heat shimmer through her. "I suppose now's as good a time as any to tell you I'm also a newspaper reporter at the *Denver Post*." He bowed his head slightly. "Andy Branigan."

Good thing she was sitting down because her entire body went limp. *Reporter. Denver Post.*

She pressed her suddenly moist fingers against the cool, slick Formica. She'd worked hard these past few years to live down "Renegade Remington" but she might as well kiss off all that do-gooding if this guy penned a story about her escape to Maiden Falls. She could see it now. How she'd been seen wearing lingerie, trying to bribe her way into a remote honeymoon hotel with no G.D. in sight...

Oh God, *Maiden Falls.*

Before, she'd thought it funny to run away and be a fallen maiden, but this guy had the power to make such a label sound real. Forget Renegade Remington. Next she'd be pegged Randy Remington. Raunchy Remington. God knew what else a reporter could do with an *R*.

She eased in a steadying breath. Except maybe, just maybe, all this fretting was moot. Maybe he didn't know who she was.

"Hey, not to worry," he said, wiping his greasy fingers on a napkin. "I won't tell."

"Tell what?" she asked tightly.

"That you're Daphne Remington, of the Denver Remingtons, set to marry the legal maverick and soon-to be gubernatorial candidate G. D. McCormick." He glanced at the four-carat diamond on her finger.

Her mouth went dry. "You recognized me on the news..."

"No, back at the hotel actually. The TV shot cinched it, though, mainly from the look of horror on your face as you recognized yourself on the screen. You're transparent, you know that?"

"Goes with my see-through attire," she muttered, not bothering to hide the irritation in her voice.

"Hey, I'm not here to betray you."

"Words are cheap."

"I guess a rich girl would know."

She narrowed her eyes. "How dare you."

"Sorry. But you're assuming I'm out to hurt you. Give a guy a chance."

"You're a reporter. I'm a Remington. Do the math." It was time to leave, get away before anything else she said or did was smeared across tomorrow's news. Damn, if her cell phone worked up here in the mountains, she'd call one of her pals in Vail or Breckenridge and say, "Pick me up! Get me out of here!"

As she slipped off her stool, he caught her arm.

"Daphne," he said, his cocky attitude gone, replaced by a seriousness that surprised her. "If I wanted to write a fast, flashy piece on the 'Runaway Remington' I could have easily phoned it in already. Tell you the truth, when I first saw you, that sure as hell crossed my mind. But I didn't do it. As I followed you over here, I decided on a better proposition. A decent one."

"Let go of me."

Andy did, reluctantly. *I shouldn't have grabbed her like that.* Hell, he never forcefully made a woman stay put—if anything, on several occasions *he'd* been the one making a beeline for the nearest exit. "Please. Hear me out. Besides, you don't have transportation, so where you gonna go?"

Her eyes widened slightly. "How do you know?"

"No Jags or Beemers parked nearby." He smiled.

She didn't.

But she also didn't leave.

"Here's the deal," he said, leaning closer, bringing their faces level. He hadn't noticed before the flecks of gold buried in her hazel eyes. "Months ago, the *Post* reserved a room for me at the inn where I'd stay while writing a piece on Colorado honeymoon hotels—it's part of a series that's running throughout May, in time for June brides and all that. What I'd like to do, if you're willing of course, is also use this weekend to interview you, write a story about whatever happened to Renegade Remington...why she ran away on the eve of her wedding—"

"I didn't run away!"

"High heels in the Rockies? No luggage?

"Do you realize what the *Post* did to me?"

Taking in her suddenly ashen face, he felt a flash of remorse for following her in here. If he'd learned anything since losing his grandfather a year ago, it was that life is too short. Sure, Andy was tough-minded—most people called him worse things—but that didn't mean he hadn't done his share of soul searching lately, trying to figure out what mattered in this crazy world. Often he'd wondered if his granddad had been right—that, bottom line, what truly mattered was how people treated one another.

"I'm sorry, Daphne. I shouldn't have—" No, he wouldn't back down. No reason to feel guilty because what he was offering was good, for both of them. "Haven't you ever wished a newspaper story also told your side of things?"

Her eyes widened again, and for an instant he swore he caught a look of interest.

"Because we could do that," he said, taking advantage of the moment. And he meant it. This could be very good. "It'd be a story that fleshes out the real Daphne Remington, her thoughts and options—"

"People are more interested in G.D.'s."

Andy paused. "Sure, G.D. You can talk up his political ambitions, agenda, whatever." Maybe she brought up the idea, but she didn't look so happy with it. "Plus you'll have two whole days of anonymity in Maiden Falls."

Damn if her whole face didn't light up on that one.

So *that* was it.

Forget G.D. She wanted a few days of freedom. Funny, that was the one thing money couldn't buy, not in this zoom lens, Internet world where people were ravenous to see into and hear about the high and mighty. He could take off for hikes, concerts or just a cup of java in the sunshine and nobody gave a damn that Andy Branigan was taking some time to enjoy himself. But for someone like Daphne Remington, such outings invited peering eyes, busybodies...

Reporters.

"Look, I don't want to pressure you." He stood, pulled a wad of money out of his pocket. "It's your choice. I already have my work cut out for me writing the honeymoon piece on the Inn at Maiden Falls. Just thought it'd be beneficial to you, and for me, to write this other piece."

He stood, taking his sweet time to count out a few bills.

"No one at the *Post* ever seemed interested in my side of things..."

He looked up. "What? Oh, right, you probably had one of those tomcat reporters only interested in making a name for himself."

"Unlike you."

"I knew if we talked a little longer, you'd understand me better." He cocked her a grin. "Hey," he said, lowering his voice. "My deal is a two-way street. Something for you, something for me. Besides, the only place I'm a tomcat is in..."

He stopped himself. *Don't blow it, Andy. It's a soda fountain, you jerk, not a pick-up bar. Which the lady's already pointed out.*

He glanced at the plate, debating if he should eat those last few fries. Hated to waste them.

"Something for you?" she asked. "Like what? Money?"

"Sure. Money."

"Liar."

He did a double take.

"You're transparent, too, you know," she said softly. "You want me to open up, then let's have you go first. Tell me, Mr. Sweet Talkin' Guy, what it is you really want."

And he thought he was the cut-to-the-chase, tell-it-like-it-is reporter. "It's not sex, if that's what you're thinking—"

"Please. You're a good-looking, charming guy but I seriously doubt you've ever had to concoct a let-me-interview you story to get laid. You, the tomcat in bed."

Damn if heat didn't flood his face. Normally *he* was the one who made the opposite sex blush.

The tension between them had shifted. He felt off-balance, but even more surprising, he felt that he was *not* the one in control.

Problem was, he never discussed his dream. Didn't

like to open up like that to people. But at the moment, he wanted to talk about *anything* other than tomcats and sex and, Lordy Lordy, how this woman and her peekaboo lace and renegade attitude would undoubtedly be hot between the sheets...

"I want to write a book," he said hoarsely, followed by a long, cold drink of lime phosphate.

"What about?"

He set down the glass, cleared his throat. "History."

"*You* want to write a book on *history*?" She pursed her lips, obviously realizing she'd just insulted him. "Sorry. I mean, I figured you'd write something like..."

"Hunter S. Thompson?"

She gave a little shrug.

Andy leaned forward, his hand sliding next to hers with the movement. Her skin was soft, warm, and he wondered where on her body she dabbed that rose scent.

"Don't judge a book by its cover," he said huskily. "Underneath this secondhand fleece jacket and ten-year-old tie-dyed T beats the heart of a guy who loves this land and its history and wants to do it justice."

The way she stared at him, her eyes shining with surprise and understanding, made him wonder if she'd been misjudged so often it took her aback to be accused of the same.

After a moment, she whispered, "What's your room like? I mean..."

"Where will we sleep?"

She paused, then nodded.

"We'll sleep separately. Hey, this is business. I'm not fool enough to do something that would result in a sexual harassment lawsuit against the *Post* because one of its reporters crossed the line."

Shut up, Andy. As Shakespeare might have said, "The man doth protest too much," because all Andy could think about was crossing the line, running his hands through those silky curls, caressing her skin, inhaling sweet lungfuls of Dulcinea.

But he couldn't. And wouldn't.

"It's a fancy honeymoon hotel, so the room's gotta have some kind of couch I can sleep on," he continued. Probably one of those "love seat" numbers that would require his knocking back plenty of aspirin after folding his six-two frame into a pretzel for an entire night. "You can have the bed."

Daphne chewed on her bottom lip. No one else knew who she was. And Andy wouldn't dare blow her identity. Or make a wrong move. After all, he needed her for the interview. Which meant her idea for a last-chance weekend where she could be free, anonymous, was *this* close to being a reality...

On the bus ride up, she'd even thought about visiting the old mining site, less than a mile away, where her great-great-great-great-grandfather Charles had staked his claim. His former shanty was now a fine Victorian home, filled with family artifacts she hadn't seen in years. Maybe if she visited the exact spot where her ancestor had experienced the most happiness, well, who knew? Some of it might rub off on her, too.

Even if she ignored the emotional reasons she wanted to stay, there was a darn good practical one. The tour bus didn't return until late tomorrow afternoon. Which meant unless she could finagle a ride back to Denver, she was stuck in Maiden Falls for the next twenty-four hours.

She looked into Andy's eyes, seeing something different in their cool-blue depths. Tenderness. Compassion, maybe.

She gave herself a mental shake. *The guy's a reporter, for God's sake.*

But he hadn't phoned in a story on her, which he could have done easily. He'd approached her with a business proposition, one that would benefit both of them.

She felt again that rush of exhilaration she'd had earlier when she'd seen the tour bus, imagined this escape. Oh, how she yearned to be impulsive again, to jump into life and experience it fully before society's rules, her family's expectations and G.D.'s "constructive criticism" stifled every such whim.

Daphne tapped her glass against his drink. "To not judging books by their covers."

"BELLE'S ROOM," Daphne said, reading the brass plaque on the door of the second-floor room at the inn. "And what is this saying underneath? 'Never fold a good hand'?"

Andy swiped his card in the lock. The room hadn't been ready when he'd checked in, so he hadn't seen it yet. He hoped all that frilly, lacy, bleeding-heart crap was confined to that historical parlor downstairs. Otherwise, a guy could OD on froufrou if he stayed here too long.

"This room is named after Belle Bulette," he said, "one of the ladies of the evening who worked here from around 1891 until that fatal gas leak in 1895—the one that took all the shady ladies' lives."

"All of them?"

"Even a judge, they say, who'd been having a late-night drink with the madam."

With a click, the door opened. "Besides being a working girl, Belle was also a sharpshooter and gambler. She took men's money both at the gambling tables and in the bedroom." Andy gestured for Daphne to enter.

"Enterprising woman," Daphne murmured, stepping inside. She stopped abruptly. "Oh, excuse us!"

"What?" Andy looked over Daphne's shoulder.

She paused, then gestured toward the smoky mirror that covered the wall behind the brass four-poster bed. "I could have sworn I saw the reflection of..." Her voice trailed off as she shifted her gaze to the bay window seat across the room.

"What is it?"

"A woman," Daphne whispered. A chill washed over her. "Sitting on that ledge, taking a sip from a flask."

Late-afternoon light filtered through the gauzy curtains on the bay windows. Andy glanced back at the mirror. Thanks to its hazy tint and the minimal light in the room, his and Daphne's features were indecipherable. All he could really see was the color of their hair. Hers, dark, almost black in this muted light. His, red. Reminded him of what his granddad had always said before a game of checkers. *Smoke before fire.*

Daphne glanced at Andy. "She seemed so real... then nothing..."

"There's hardly any light," Andy said, searching the wall. "Easy to imagine things." He flicked a switch. An overhead electric chandelier came to life, infusing the room with a bright glow. He looked around. The brass bed was big, and he didn't know if he'd ever seen a chandelier in a bedroom, but everything else was sedate, tasteful. Didn't smack of frou-frou. A guy could breathe in this room, relax.

"Except I'm not one to imagine things," Daphne murmured. "I pretty much call it as I see it." She frowned. "You're not going to smoke in here, are you?"

He held a pack of cigarettes he'd just extracted from his pullover pocket. "Uh, let me think about it." He looked briefly up, then back down. "Yes." He popped the filter-tip into his mouth.

"There's a No Smoking sign downstairs."

"Good place for it." He struck a match and drew it to the tip of his cigarette. The scent of sulfur stung the air.

Daphne snatched the cigarette from his lips. "No."

He shook out the match. "Hey, who invited whom to this room?"

"You want me to turn you in? Keep the room for myself?"

He gave a double take. "You can't do that—"

"Watch me."

He was watching all right. Watching that dare-me glint in her eyes. The imperial tilt of her chin.

The lady was a handful.

Fortunately, he knew how to handle handfuls.

"Sure," he said, ambling over to the love seat—looks like he called that one. Hopefully, the aspirin was close by. "Go ahead and report me. I'll say you broke in and tried to steal my room. After that little gimme-a-room-or-else routine you pulled at the front desk earlier, I have a feeling they'll buy my story over yours in, oh, the space of a heartbeat?" He sat down and stretched out his legs.

She watched him through slitted eyes. "You wouldn't say that."

"*You* watch *me*." He stroked his fingers over plush velvet. "I believe the cops call it breaking and entering. The news of your alleged crime would be on the Internet faster than a giga-minute. Reporters would be flocking here like adrenaline-crazed swallows to Capistrano."

"Aren't you taking this a bit too far? Adrenaline-crazed birds, good grief." With a sanctimonious sigh, she lobbed the cigarette back to him. "Go ahead, die of lung cancer."

"Cheery sort, aren't you?" Eyeing a wicker trash can, he dunked the cig in one smooth toss. "But I'll spare you the secondhand smoke. Believe it or not, I *can* be a gentleman."

"Thought you were a tomcat." Daphne laughed. "You're calculating, cocky—"

"But sexy. Admit it."

He caught the stain of pink on her cheeks.

So she does think I'm sexy.

A hint of lilacs wafted past and he suddenly thought about that old photo in the downstairs album. "Belle was a renegade, too."

Daphne arched an eyebrow. "I'm not Renegade Remington anymore..." She turned away to check herself in a mirror, but not before Andy caught a look of sadness shading her face. Did she secretly like the nickname because it fit who she truly was?

Rather than pursue that line of thought, he opted to share what he'd read about Belle Bulette. "When Belle arrived in Maiden Falls," Andy said, standing, "she never said where she came from. But I think Belle Bulette—and this is purely speculation—is actually a play on her nickname when she lived in Tombstone, which was Bonnie Bullet. She was quite a gal. Smart, stubborn, fearless. High-tempered, too."

For a moment, he wasn't sure if he'd just described Belle or Daphne.

But he was sure he just heard her stomach growl. "Hungry?"

"Sure."

Probably famished but won't admit it. "Stories circulated that Belle—well, when she was Bonnie—shot a man in a poker game in Tombstone—"

"Shot?"

"Yes, as in killed."

"Why?"

"He'd cheated at cards."

The lights flickered.

"Did you see that?" asked Andy.

Daphne, who'd been inspecting the satin bedspread looked up. "Probably the wind."

He looked out the window. Leaves on the aspens were fluttering, the gentle movement from breezes, hardly winds. "Anyway, after she shot him, she slipped out of Tombstone, never to be heard of again."

"But you said she came here—"

"I'm surmising, but I think I'm right on. Bonnie and Belle were working girls, expert gamblers and both carried an ivory-handled Colt .44 Peacemaker. Unfortunately, there are no good photographs of Bonnie, although people wrote about her waist-length auburn hair. Her lover, a gambler and an educated man named Drake Galloway, always carried a lock of it. It was found in his pocket when he died. His last words were that he loved her."

A glass decanter on a corner table rattled.

Daphne blinked at the table, then turned her attention back to Andy. "Did you hear that?"

He shrugged. "Probably the wind." Ignoring Daphne's double take, he crossed the room and lifted the receiver from the phone on the nightstand. "What kind of pizza do you like?"

"Tell room service I'd like a broiled skinless chicken breast and a salad. Lemon, no dressing."

"Sorry, baby, but this reporter is saving his per diem for a nice shot of something warm and intoxicating later. Meanwhile, we're using my gift certificate to order pizza." After asking the hotel operator to connect him to Pete's Pizza, Andy said "I'd like to order a large, deep-dish pizza, extra cheese—"

"No extra cheese for me."

"—pepperoni, sausage—"

"I want vegetables."

"—and throw on some onions. We're at the Inn at Maiden Falls, Belle's Room on the second floor."

Daphne rolled her eyes, wishing she hadn't spent her last twenty-five dollars on some face cream and a toothbrush at the drugstore so she'd have the means to buy a salad. But when she'd been tempted to use one of her credit cards for some other essentials—like mascara, lipstick—she'd stopped after realizing her whereabouts could be traced if she used plastic.

Although she seriously doubted her family—or G.D., who was out of town—would notice her absence, she didn't want to risk it. Especially now that she was rooming with a *Denver Post* reporter!

Andy sauntered to the door, put his hand on the knob. "They have port, cheese and crackers in the lobby about now. I'll get some for us to nosh on before the pizza arrives."

"Cheese, crackers, pizza," muttered Daphne.

"Hey, three of the four food groups!" Andy said, quickly shutting the door behind him.

BELLE TOOK another swig of whiskey, then stuck her flask in the waistband of her drawers. *Hellfire and...* She bit off the curse, hoping Miss Arlotta hadn't caught the thought. Although most of the girls had had a colorful vocabulary when they were alive, Miss Arlotta wanted them to be more pristine-like as they earned their way to the Big Picnic in the Sky. And Belle definitely had a problem using pristine language when the healthier variety was far more satisfying.

Which was what she felt like doing right now, cursing a streak after being stuck in her room with two *pals*, not lovers! She might as well kiss off her golden opportunity to earn the all-important last bedpost notch.

She watched the dark-haired woman saunter around the room, checking out the chandelier, the stocked goods in what they called a minibar.

Hmmm, maybe that last notch was still possible...

Heck, Belle had been a skilled gambler because she never backed down from a challenge. Now that she thought about it, being stuck with a couple of pals was like upping the stakes. If she could make these two "feel the heat," Belle could earn a big fat gold star worth several bedpost notches at least. That kind of glorious accomplishment could advance her, fast, to the "Big P."

Feel the heat? She grinned. Not a bad idea.

She pointed at the thermostat, waggled her finger, then floated to the door. While things got cookin' up here, she'd see what tactics she might use with Andy downstairs.

Plus, she was curious as hell—heck—how he'd guessed about her past as Bonnie. Nobody in all the time she'd been haunting this hotel—nearly a hundred and nine years—had ever put it together that she was really Bonnie Bullet from Tombstone.

Which meant nobody had ever known about her history with Drake Galloway, either.

Their secrets—some precious, one painfully tender—Belle had been prepared to carry by herself into eternity. She hadn't expected some ruffian to check into her room with information she'd never known....

That Drake's last words were about loving her.

Blinking back a surprising wave of sadness and nostalgia, Belle glided out of the room, barely aware of the decanter rattling in her wake.

3

A FEW MINUTES later, Andy stepped into the lobby and inched past a young couple kissing feverishly, their bodies hovering over a tray of assorted cheeses on a side table. If they writhed a little lower, they could do serious damage to the Camembert.

For the most part, Andy viewed himself as an easy-going kinda guy—even if others disagreed with his self-image—but he did have two pet peeves: people who took love to the gooey stage and good food being wasted. The latter was due to his growing up economically strapped. Which wasn't a bad thing. When you're counting pennies to see if you have enough to buy day-old bread, you develop an appreciation for free, wholesome fare, especially the load-up-on-as-much-as-you-can-eat variety.

The girl came up for air, sighed heavily, then fell back into her guy for more kissing and moaning.

"Excuse me," Andy muttered, grabbing a plate and making a dive for the cheese before it was crushed—or worse, melted—underneath the overheated honeymooners. He piled on some Brie, Camembert and crackers. Juggling the plate with one hand, he reached for the bottle of port and paused.

The scent of lilacs again.

He looked around, but the only people in the room were Andy and the lip-locked lovers.

A rasping sound, a gentle scraping against wood, caught his attention.

He eyed the spread—plates of cheese, crackers, fruit and assorted utensils, cups and condiments. Next to a salt shaker, a blue-and-white box of cards seemed to move...almost imperceptibly so.

Right. Moving cards.

Next I'll be seeing floating cheese.

He sloshed some port into a glass and tossed back a sip, letting the rich, plum-scented liquid warm his throat.

The couple teetered, brushed against him.

Andy gave his head a small shake, wondering why some men succumbed to such ridiculous, public displays of needy gooey-ness. *Get a room, buddy. The one you're paying for.*

BELLE LEANED against the table, observing Andy. *Cynical ruffian, aren't ya?*

She tapped her fingers on the box of cards, debating whether to give it another little shove. But she sensed it was a lost cause. Andy was overly worked up about that kissing couple, whose ghostly gal—hmm, was it Glory?—was a shoo-in for a bedpost notch this weekend.

Belle looked back at Andy, wondering if he was

aware that when he got irritated, his neck flushed almost to the color of his hair.

She'd never been one to show her emotions like that. In life, she couldn't afford to because a good gambler was a master of the placid face. However, Belle certainly related to Andy's cynicism because she'd been a lot like that herself. How many times had her beloved Drake said in his lazy New Orleans drawl, "Darlin' gal, you make a skeptic look ambivalent."

She'd always defended herself by reminding him that a woman on her own in the frontier had to be not only tough, but a good "businessman," too. And that's what she'd saved her money for, to own her own business one day. A high-class gambling hall—a place even fancier than Denver's Palace Theater, which Bat Masterson had acquired about that time.

Belle sighed. Funny to recall how money once drove her. Now it was notches.

She watched Andy juggle the plate of food with one hand while lifting two glasses in the other.

Not bad with his hands.

She'd keep that in mind, later, when things heated up. She smiled to herself, thinking how she'd already kicked off part of the "heated" before she left her room...

Belle stroked the deck of cards one last time, willing the idea of strip poker to occur to Andy. It took more effort to plant the idea because of that passionate couple's energy. True love was a wild force to be reckoned with, a fact Belle hadn't known until after she'd left the earthly realm. If humans knew how powerful and far-reaching love's effects were, they might choose to do many things differently.

Andy suddenly glanced upward, as though startled. Then he slowly grinned, an unholy twinkle in his eyes.

Bull's-eye. Belle floated away, pleased with her newest ability to send thoughts. Sometimes it worked with dreams, too, a trick she was perfecting.

Andy headed into the foyer, humming a tune, and Belle followed. One peculiar thing about being a ghost—peculiar for Belle, anyway—she felt vibrations from *everything.* A tree, a sunrise, even a wish. A human singing, even humming, was extraordinarily sensual. She floated up the stairs, enveloping herself in the sensations of Andy's melodic, deep voice.

Drake had had a good singing voice, too.

A funny ache filled her as she again recalled Andy's words. "His last words were that he loved her."

She swallowed, hard, pushing down an old regret. She'd left Tombstone without saying goodbye. Belle had always figured it was easier that way. If the law had badgered Drake about her whereabouts or tried to liquor him up to spill the beans, he honestly would have had no information.

Then, a month later, when she discovered she was... Well, going back meant dealing with the law, jail time at the minimum, so she kept moving on. Over the years, she figured Drake had forgotten her, married, had his own family. She never knew that her Drake had died thinking of her....

Loving her.

If she still had a beating heart, it would surely break.

JUGGLING the plate and glasses of port, Andy knocked the toe of his boot against the bottom of his room door.

"Locked out?" asked a woman's voice.

Andy looked over his shoulder. The hotel manager, dressed in a pink and orange floor-length dress that made her look like a huge floating sunset, stood in the hallway.

At the same time, Daphne called out from behind the door, "Who is it?"

The manager swerved her gaze to the door.

"It's me," Andy said. He cleared his throat, avoiding the manager's gaze. "Your husband."

He wasn't sure if his response was a stroke of genius or stupidity, but it seemed far better to be *married* in a honeymoon hotel than to appear he'd gone out and *picked up* someone.

Which, technically, he'd done, of course.

The chain lock scraped, the door creaked open.

Daphne leaned against the doorjamb, dressed in those cargo pants topped with that green lingerie number. Through the sheer fabric, he saw the circles of her dark nipples. His insides contracted, suckerpunched with hot need.

"Finally!" She fanned herself with her manicured

hand. "I'm so hot—" She stopped mid-sentence and stared, openmouthed, at the manager.

Who stared back, blinking rapidly.

Andy quickly stepped inside, hoping to hell he didn't drop the plate or drinks and make a bigger fiasco than the one brewing on his doorstep. Whenever he found himself struggling with a news story, he threw on more facts. He'd do that now, too. Not that they were *real* facts, but he needed to fabricate *something*. Hell, what better time for sweet talkin'? He was going to be here for the entire weekend—requesting access to rooms, stats, historical trivia—it would be damn beneficial not to make an enemy of the manager.

"My, uh, wife arrived after I did, not knowing I'd already checked in." Good thing he'd stood out of sight of the manager when she and Daphne had had their go-around at the registration desk earlier. Afterward, the manager had left so quickly—scurrying down the hallway that led to the back of the hotel— she'd missed Andy following Daphne to the drugstore across the street.

With a confused expression, the manager said to Andy, "But...she could have mentioned your name, said she was your wife..."

She could have kept her jacket on, too, and not ramrodded my libido answering the door in that next-to-nothing piece of fluff. "She'd been traveling for days—"

"Day," Daphne corrected.

"From *Denver?*" The manager frowned. "We're only an hour's drive from there."

"She...walked."

The owner looked at Daphne's heels.

"From the bus to the hotel." Daphne gave a little shrug. "I'm great in heels."

An image of her wearing nothing but those heels seared through Andy's mind. "We need to go now," he croaked, nudging the door closed with his toe.

"You're married," the manager said, leaning forward to peer through the closing door, "but travel *separately?*"

"We travel apart," Daphne said, her voice rising, "in case one of us is in a fatal accident. The other will survive. We do it for the children—"

The door shut with a resounding click.

Andy paused, then turned and gave Daphne a long look. "Fatal accident? Survival for the children? Cheery sort, aren't you?" He set the plate and glasses on a corner table.

"I was making our story legitimate. Which someone had to do because the *reporter* in the bunch was losing it."

He turned. "Excuse me?"

She swiped a strand of hair out of her eyes. "I'm your *wife?* Who traveled *days* from Denver on *foot?* Hello?"

He opened his mouth to say something intelligent, possibly profound, but his mind turned into a vast wasteland as he stared at the strip of black lace that fringed the silky green. Through the intricate mesh of black, he caught peeks of creamy skin and the hint of cleavage.

"If you want me to make sense," he rasped, "keep your jacket on."

She shifted her weight from one high heel to the other. "It got unbearably hot in here after you left."

"Thought it'd be the other way around."

"What?"

"That it gets unbearably hot when I'm *in* the room, not when I'm gone."

She sucked in a breath that made her breasts press sinfully against the fabric. "You're impudent."

"So I've heard." He'd be something else in a moment, something worse, like grossly inappropriate or plain ol' I-said-I'd-be-good-but-let's-be-bad-instead if he kept staring at those perky green-draped mounds.

She's right. It's hot in here.

Andy walked like an automaton to the thermostat. He punched a button with a down arrow several times. "You cranked it up to ninety."

"I never touched it! Didn't even know it was there. The thermostat is white against a white wall."

She had a point. He'd only known where it was because he'd seen it earlier while searching for the light switch. Still, it hadn't been set on ninety when they'd first come into the room—maybe Daphne had brushed against it, accidentally pushed the button. Although what she'd be doing brushing her body against a wall was a thought best left unthought.

"Okay," he said, turning around. "I reset it to seventy. It'll cool down in a moment—"

For a moment he'd thought he'd gone snow-blind. "What's—?"

"Oh." Daphne gestured toward the sheet dangling from the ceiling, its bottom edge falling in a line down the middle of the bed. "I thought it would be helpful to divide the bed. You know, your side and my side."

He looked up at the ceiling, where one end of the sheet was attached to the chandelier, the other tied around one of the track lights at the top of the mirrored wall. He'd been so caught up in the scene at the door, then dealing with the temperature, he'd missed the...

"Sheet?" He gave his head a disbelieving shake. "You hung a *sheet* to ensure I stay on my side of the bed? You could've drawn a line with a black marker down the bedspread and saved yourself some effort."

"I thought it'd be helpful if we didn't see each other."

He stared at her, amazed at her line of reasoning. "When I'm asleep," he finally said, "my eyes are closed. Don't need no sheet, baby, not to see you." He tugged off his fleece jacket and tossed it over a chair. It was hot in here, and growing hotter by the minute even *with* the thermostat turned down. "Anyway, I already told you I'd sleep on the couch."

"Which part of you? Upper or lower? It's not that big."

"The floor, then." He looked back at Daphne, who

was standing spread-eagled, her fists on her hips. Golden light from the chandelier gilded her body. And he'd thought the lingerie top would be his undoing? Ha. It'd be the buttery light pouring over her arms and legs and glinting sinfully off the zipper of her pants.

"It's hardwood," Daphne said.

"Huh?"

"The floor. It's hardwood."

With Herculean effort, he raised his gaze to hers, wondering how it would taste to lick warm, melted butter off her naked skin. "I've slept hard before."

"What?"

"Hardwood." He cleared his throat. "I mean I've slept on hardwood floors before. I'll steal a blanket and a pillow. It'll be fine." *It'll be hell, curled up on the floor, knowing your buttery body is mere feet away....*

"Don't be silly. We'll sleep together in the bed. I trust you."

Glad one of us does. "I need a drink," he croaked, walking stiff-kneed to the table and picking up a glass of port. Maybe he should take a cold shower...for the rest of the evening.

Behind him, he heard Daphne talking, something about the layout of the room, or maybe it was the bed, and he forced himself not to fixate on the word *lay*. In fact, not to fixate on anything she said...or how she looked...or if she liked butter.

I should've taken Donita up on her offer. Donita was the new gossip columnist at the *Post*. A little round, a lot hyper and unafraid to proposition a man outright. He'd discovered that last week at the local watering hole, the Supreme Court Bar, when she inched her stockinged foot into his crotch under the table.

Problem was, as much as Andy had a reputation with the ladies, he had *some* integrity. For example, he didn't fool around with co-workers. And he didn't bed a woman just because she let him know she was available. Or could skillfully wriggle her toes.

Of course, tonight, he was damn close to *sharing* a bed with a woman who had made it clear she was very unavailable. Even if she changed her mind, the last thing Andy Branigan needed was to invoke the wrath of the possible next governor of the state.

He eased out a long, slow breath. *This is going to be a long, long weekend.*

He lifted the second glass, turned and offered it to Daphne. "Have a drink."

Across the room, something on the nightstand caught his eye.

A deck of playing cards? They hadn't been there before, had they?

"Thank you," Daphne said, accepting the glass.

Andy pulled his attention back to her, unsure if the sensation skittering down his spine was hot or cold.

DAPHNE TOWELED OFF her face, looking at her reflection in the bathroom mirror, wishing she hadn't spent all of her cash. *I should have bought the less expensive cream so I could purchase some foundation, too.* She glared at the smattering of freckles across her nose which she'd always hated. Made her look like Rebecca of Sunnybrook Farm. All she needed was a pair of overalls to complete the look.

Andy said I was transparent.

She arched an eyebrow. Oh, really? Maybe he saw her passing emotions, or in a minute these damn freckles, but no way was she so transparent that he'd see down to her deepest, most private thoughts or dreams. Those she'd learned long ago to keep hidden.

She opened the door and stepped into the bedroom.

And halted.

If she didn't know better, she'd swear the room was lit by candles, not electricity. She glanced up at the chandelier. Strange. The bulbs seemed dimmer. Yet she remembered distinctly that Andy had flicked a switch, not a dimmer, to turn on the light.

"Feel better?" asked Andy. He was propped against some bunched pillows on the bed, his fingers on the laptop keyboard.

"Felt refreshing to wash my face."

"Good." He returned his attention to the computer.

Good? As in good, glad you feel refreshed? Or you look good even though I can count the number of freckles on your face all the way from across the room, Rebecca?

She squeezed shut her eyes. *It doesn't matter. This is my weekend, not a date.* But when she thought about Andy, something hot and intense flared within her.

Okay, forget the "this is my weekend" rationale. What he

thinks about me matters. But not enough to actually
something about it. *It's not as though I've forgotten I'*.
engaged.

She fiddled with the ring on her hand, wondering
when it had started to feel so heavy.

She opened her eyes and looked at Andy. His head
was bent, a lock of golden-red hair falling over his
brow. When he focused intently, the way he was now,
he didn't seem so cocky. More boyish. studious. The
kind of guy who would read a literary masterpiece
cover to cover. She liked how he channeled his energy,
losing himself in his concentration.

She shuddered involuntarily, imaging what it
would be like to be the recipient of that kind of intense, focused energy while making love.

*Thinking about sex is the last thing you need to be doing
right now.* Besides, wasn't she the one who had been
determined to keep things proper by hanging that
wall of a sheet?

Andy looked up. "What're you thinking about?"

Sex. You. "Working on the honeymoon hotel story?"
she asked, her voice doing that breathy thing again.

"A bit. Also framing the interview questions I want
to ask you."

"Like—?"

Andy looked at her, his gaze skimming down her
body, back to her eyes. "You put your jacket back on."

"That's not a question." *I look good to him.*

"Want to...take off your jacket?"

eally good to him. "This doesn't sound like an in-
view."

"No, but it's a question."

She giggled. Not an oh-that's-funny giggle, but a
wheezy oh-my-toes-are-curling kind of giggle. The
way she had behaved when she was thirteen and
eighth-grade stud Keith Jones had graced her with
one of his bad-boy grins.

Andy's eyes flashed with interest. One side of his
mouth kicked up in a saucy, gotcha grin that made
Keith Jones a blur of ancient history. When Andy gave
her a possessive, slow once-over, her body heat sky-
rocketed.

In a flash—as though she were looking at a photograph—she saw the bed without the dividing sheet,
the covers tangled, two naked bodies entwined....

She gasped, realizing it was her and Andy.

The image faded, replaced with Andy sitting there,
staring at her with a look that messaged heat and sin.

The kind of look that reminded her they were alone
in this hotel room...that the door was locked....

She caught her reflection in the mirror behind the
bed. Her face was flushed, her hair a mass of wild
curls. And that smile...she'd never seen herself smile
like that. Her eyes glistening, her lips curved as
though suppressing a wicked secret....

Seeing herself like that, looking alive and excited, it
hit Daphne how long it'd been since she'd really felt
that way. She realized that what she was experiencing
in this moment—this hot, sizzling moment—was

more real than anything she'd experienced in a long, long time; all her do-gooding these past few years was a sham.

Because, truth be told, she *was* a renegade. She loved a life free of restraints. Loved to be wild, to indulge herself in life's exhilarating journeys. But she'd caved in somewhere along the line, tried to be what everybody told her to be. And in a rush of understanding she suddenly knew why.

She'd given up.

She'd given up believing there ever would be more. Believing there would be another chance to embrace life wholeheartedly without fear or guilt. Believing she would ever meet a man whose smile was a portal to adventure and joy and passion...

"Andy," she whispered, yanking open her jacket. "Come here...."

4

KNOCK knock knock.

"The door," Daphne whispered.

Andy nodded slowly, a dazed look on his face. "Door," he repeated as though he'd never heard the word before. He dragged his hand through his hair. "Right, *door*." He pushed aside the laptop.

Belle flew off the love seat. *No!*

Andy rolled off the bed, stood.

No! Belle soared across the room, willing thoughts into his mind. *Don't open the door! She wants you, you fool!*

As though jolted by something, Andy halted. He glanced at Daphne. Their gazes held.

Good! Belle reinvoked an earlier image she'd planted in Andy's head. He and Daphne playing strip poker, her pulling that green silk chemise over her head, her naked breasts glazed with candlelight.

His lips spread in a slow smile.

Knock knock knock. "Room service with the pizza you ordered."

Andy blinked, did a double take at the door, then back at Daphne. "We want—" he scratched his chin "—the pizza, right?"

She fingered the lapel of her jacket. "Right," she whispered.

"Right." With a hard shake of his head, Andy turned away and walked through Belle toward the door.

No! Belle whirled around, somewhat dazed by the waves of desire emanating from these two, which she'd especially felt when Andy passed through her. She often had experienced the vibrations of a couple's sexual energy—a rippling through the air like heat waves. But this couple was another story! Their energy was hot, powerful—like the searing heat off a blazing bonfire.

All the more reason to get this show on the road.

Belle hovered in front of Daphne. *You must stop him!* She strained to plant a thought in Daphne's mind, images of the two of them naked in bed, making love, but Belle's thoughts seemed to hit a wall. Damn, the trick was too new. Plus, it hadn't been tested "under the gun" so to speak.

Andy approached the door, his back to the rest of the room.

Desperate to do something, *anything,* Belle flickered into materialization.

Daphne's eyes widened in alarm. She opened her mouth...

Belle raised her hands to reassure her. "Don't scream," she whispered.

Daphne's saucer-wide eyes remained transfixed on Belle.

Knock knock knock.

"I'm coming, hold your horses," called out Andy.

As though shocked back into reality by the *real* noises, Daphne started. She pointed a shaking finger at Belle. "Gho-gho—"

"I'm going! I'm going!" Andy said. He muttered something under his breath about women and pizza and sex.

Belle gave her head a shake. *Hell's bells. How am I supposed to salvage this mess?*

Miss Arlotta's voice blasted through the room. "What in the Sam Hill's going on in there? You're scaring that poor woman to death!"

To death? I should hope not. This place is crowded enough as it is.

Andy started to open the door.

Rapidly de-materializing, Belle leaned closer to Daphne and whispered, "You and that man are meant for each other."

Daphne stiffened, gulped a breath, then peeled off an ear-splitting shriek.

Andy jerked his gaze to Daphne. "What the—?"

A stunned-looking bellhop stood on the threshold, clutching a large cardboard box. "Pizza?" he croaked.

"Belle!" commanded Miss Arlotta. "Get your bustle up here *now!*"

Darn, dang and double tarnation. Feeling miffed and frustrated—and damn it all anyway, she *never* had been this emotional in real life—Belle stormed through the door and toward the stairs, the decanter rattling in her wake.

"I—I just felt a rush of cold air," whispered the bellhop.

Andy thought he'd also smelled lilacs again, but no way he was going to add *that* newsflash to the weirdness already going on in the room.

"Daph—" He caught himself. "Darling, are you all right?"

"No." She darted a look at the bellhop, then back to Andy. "Yes. Thought I saw..."

"A bug?" asked Andy. He'd been through this before with other women, although he'd never seen one so frightened her face appeared literally drained of blood.

"Sort of." Daphne smiled tightly. "Gone now," she said with an apologetic shrug.

Andy caught on. She didn't want to cause a scene, draw any more attention to herself because the last thing she wanted was someone identifying that shrieking woman staying in the honeymoon hotel room with a strange man as Daphne Remington.

"Let me take that," he said calmly, reaching for the pizza box.

"Di-did that thing move?" asked the bellhop, staring at the glass decanter on the table.

Andy got a firm grip on the box, determined also to keep a firm grip on his sanity. In the last few minutes, he'd been tormented with images of five-card stud and a semi-naked Daphne, having to choose between hot pizza and a hot woman—the old Andy would *never* have chosen the pizza—plus a soul-piercing scream and cold air and lilacs and...

He welcomed the box's warmth and the steamy scents of cheese and spices. Yes, much better to have chosen pizza over a woman, especially *this* woman. Enough was out of whack without adding a bunch of pissed-off Remingtons and an irate gubernatorial wanna-be into the mix. Andy needed to stay focused on his deadline and the interview. That's all that mattered.

He set the box next to the decanter on the circular marble-topped table.

The boy pointed. "Tha-that bottle. It definitely moved a few seconds ago."

"It's the wind." Andy pulled a few bills out of his pocket.

"Wind?" The boy looked at the windows. "They're closed."

"A draft, then. Underneath all this renovation and fancy interior design, you know, is a very old building."

The boy glanced up and down the hall, then leaned closer and whispered, "They say the hotel is haunted."

"Yeah, right." Andy handed the bills to the boy.

"No, really," the boy said, accepting the money. "They say the shady ladies who used to work here are *still* here."

Andy glanced over his shoulder at Daphne, who

was standing in the center of the room looking, well, as though she'd seen a ghost.

"Listen," he said, turning back to the boy, "when you buy into stuff like that, you set yourself up. It's like being afraid of anything in the world. Afraid of the dark? You'll find reasons to keep the lights on all night. It's all in your head." He glanced at the kid's name tag. "Billy, thanks for bringing the pizza to our room. Have a great night, okay?"

"Uh, sure." The boy flashed a hesitant smile, enough to show the sparkle of braces. "Have a good evening, sir."

Andy shut the door, headed across the room to where he'd tossed his pullover. He felt a little chillier, but not because of that kid saying he felt something cold. No, it was growing dusky outside. And in the mountains, temperatures dropped dramatically at night.

"Want to tell me what that scream was about?" he asked, grabbing his pullover off one of the bedposts.

"I saw something."

"So you started to say." Snaking his arms through the red fleece, he waited for more. And waited. Why was it women could sometimes talk your ear off, then turn around and make you pull information out of them. "And that something was—?"

"Nothing," she croaked. "I don't want to talk about it."

"All right," Andy said, tugging the pullover down. *She regrets coming on to me.* It didn't explain the scream, but when a woman left the topic of discussion up for grabs, well, a guy typically grabbed whatever had recently dented his male ego.

"Let's eat," he grumbled, heading back to the table. He opened the pizza box, his stomach growling at the mouthwatering scents of meat and cheese.

"*That*," he said over his shoulder, "was my stomach. Just for the record."

"Gee, thought it was the decanter rattling."

Her sense of humor was back. *Must be feeling better about whatever had been bothering her.*

"Look," he said, turning to face her. "Whatever I did to upset you, I'm sorry." He'd skip the part about her exiting the bathroom and making a move on him. When things got shaky with a lady, always best to back off, apologize. That little rule had been drilled into him by his gramps he didn't know how many times.

"You didn't upset me."

"Okay, I didn't. So, let's move on, forget about strip poker." *Damn.* "I mean, forget about whatever happened that I didn't do or did do but it didn't upset you—"

"I saw a...ghost."

We're back to that? He glanced at the decanter, back to Daphne. "It was the wi—"

"Not the wind. A ghost." She shifted her gaze toward the love seat.

"Do you—" he glanced at the empty love seat "—still see it?"

Daphne looked back at Andy. "Her."

"Her." *What the hell am I doing? Now I'm talking about it*—her—*as though it exists.*

"No, I don't. Doesn't mean she's not here still. She disappeared right in front of my eyes. But she got close, really close, and I smelled lilacs..."

Lilacs? His stomach clenched. No. *No* way he was getting sucked into this fantasy gobbledegook. If he took a deep enough breath *anywhere* in this joint, he'd probably smell lilacs. Had to be the manager's perfume, which lingered everywhere because she was everywhere, nosing around, checking up on single guys who'd picked up babes at the malt shop across the street and brought them back to their rooms for hot, unwedded sex.

Or so a guy could wish.

He cleared his throat. "You're letting those ghostly rumors get the better of you—"

"Just like a man to doubt a woman."

"Listen, Daphne, just because that kid said this hotel was haunted doesn't make it so. Hell, every hotel over fifty years old claims to be haunted. That place near Colorado Springs swears Teddy Roosevelt, rifle in hand, still roams the halls saying 'Bully for you.' Such stories drum up business. Free PR. A publicist's wet dream. Come on, let's eat."

"She said..." Daphne didn't finish her thought.

He set out the napkins, a plastic container of pepper flakes. "She?"

"The ghost."

"You like jalapeños? Hope so, because they smoth-
ered this pizza with them..."

His voice trailed off as he caught the frightened look
in Daphne's eyes. He could handle her stubbornness,
well, for the most part, but seeing that she was genu-
inely afraid—looking so damn vulnerable—took him
aback. Maybe he didn't know Daphne all that well,
but he'd bet hard-earned money this woman never let
down her guard, never trusted, which saddened him.

"I'm sorry," he murmured, straightening. "I
shouldn't make light of what you're feeling."

Daphne felt frozen to the spot on the floor she'd
been standing on for what seemed a small forever,
feeling numb from the rush of whatever the hell had
transpired these last few minutes. She had an imagination, yes. Used it in her photography all the time,
but there was seeing things and then there was *seeing*
things. And she'd never, ever, seen a vapory image of
a—a ghost?—before.

One who talked to her, no less.

But no one else in the room saw or heard the ghost.
Sure, the bellhop had repeated the rumor of this hotel
being haunted, but he didn't seem to have witnessed
anything firsthand. Oh, the decanter. Well, it had rattled before. Maybe the result of the door opening or
something heavy being moved down the hall or in another room that caused the floor to shake a little,
which in turn caused the crystal to rattle.

It's stress.

I've been under too much of it lately.

Pressure from her family, her friends, Gordo. It was stressful enough getting married. Double, triple that when it was to a political bigwig. Scrutiny had been fierce, worse than the aftermath of her infamous swan dive into the country-club pool. She was even getting nervous about doing everyday things in Denver, like having lunch with girlfriends, for fear someone would report she'd said or done something inappropriate.

Oh, for the days when all she worried about was whether spinach was stuck in her teeth.

A sickening wave of anxiety washed over her and she wondered when all of this would end. Maybe she'd wanted to run away for a weekend, but it was only a temporary fix. All that critical, suffocating attention awaited her the moment she got back home.

She squeezed her eyes shut, trying to ward off the cold foreboding.

"Daphne?"

She opened her eyes.

Andy stood before her, filling her vision, those blue eyes flashing concern.

His hand cupped her arm. "Why don't you sit down?"

"I'm okay—"

"Let me take care of you."

A protective gesture, but this close she was suddenly all too aware of the difference in their size. How he towered over her, an imposing mass of strength and masculinity. Gordo was tall, taller actually. But when he stood this close to her, she mainly felt his dominance.

With Andy, she felt his concern.

She was all too aware of other things, too. How the light caught strands of gold in his red hair. A small, jagged scar on his chin. His masculine scent.

His breath mixing with hers.

For the space of one breath...two...three...she felt her fear dissolve, seep away, replaced by the warming reassurance of Andy's shielding presence.

She nodded in agreement—not remembering exactly what the question had been—as her gaze slipped from his eyes to his lips and she suddenly found herself wondering what it'd be like to kiss him. *Sweetly spicy* came her answer.

Desire welled deep within her, tender and soft, primal and coarse, and for a dizzying moment, she wanted nothing more than to be in this man's arms. To explore his warmth, drown in his scent, burn at his touch...

The word *lovers* seemed to weave through the room and surround them, like a satin caress.

"Sit down?" Andy repeated.

"Yes," she whispered, taking his hand. "Oh, yes..."

MISS ARLOTTA, an imperious eyebrow arched high, crossed her arms over her ample chest—the satin bodice making a soft rasping sound with the movement— and said, "Two black marks."

"Two?" Belle crossed her arms as well. "One. For cussing."

The older woman, lounging back on her favorite settee, shook her head of pale-blond curls. "Belle, darlin', this isn't a negotiation. You cussed *and* you materialized inappropriately. Two black marks."

Not a negotiation? Like heck it isn't. Deep down, Belle knew that just as she and Miss Arlotta had loved business in life, they still loved it. And part of being a savvy businesswoman was being a quick-thinking negotiator.

Of course, sometimes negotiations needed some help...

Belle looked over at the judge, reading a book in the corner. He was the only one who could override a decision of Miss Arlotta's, partly because of his stellar reputation as a fair and honorable judge, partly because he had the key to Miss Arlotta's heart. Then *and* now. The evening of the gas leak, he'd been enjoying a nightcap with Miss Arlotta in her office, the two of them dressed in their evening finest after a late-night dinner. Now he bided his afterlife at the inn, communicating his judicial expertise when necessary and loving his lady—"Lotta" as he called her—until all the girls passed on to the Big Picnic in the Sky.

Because, as they all knew, only when all the girls had redeemed themselves could the judge and Miss Arlotta move on, too.

When he didn't look up from his book, a silent sign

that he was leaving this decision solely to Miss Arlotta, Belle turned back to the madam.

"I'm willing to 'fess up to the cussing—"

"No need to, Belle, I heard you."

"But as to the other matter, they'd already crossed
the threshold into my room when I materialized."

"True. But you frightened that poor woman to
death. What's her name?"

"Daphne."

"Daphne. Need I repeat that golden rule?" Miss Arlotta waggled her fingers and a scroll appeared in her
hands. Belle had never figured out how that little trick
was done, but then she could spend the rest of eternity
trying to figure out everything Miss A. knew.

Miss Arlotta pulled open the scroll, humming as she
scanned the paper. "We are here," Miss Arlotta read,
"to help them find pleasure in each other, not scare the
livin' daylights out of 'em by fading in and out or
showing up in bits and pieces at the wrong time."

"I didn't show up in bits and pieces."

Miss Arlotta rolled up the scroll and flung it aside. It
disappeared into nothingness. "But you scared the
livin' daylights out of her, so it's one black mark for
cussing, one for frightening."

"But, it wasn't intentional! I'm doing everything in
my power to get that last notch, to be finally free, *despite* being stuck with two people who were strangers
only yesterday might I add!"

Miss Arlotta cast a knowing look at Belle. "I know,

darlin', that it hasn't always been easy for you. Maybe if the child..."

Belle felt an acute sense of loss, as though what had happened were only yesterday. Only Miss Arlotta knew the whole story, and they had a ladies' agreement always to keep it that way.

"That was a long time ago." And for a moment, Belle honest to God thought she'd cry, something spirits couldn't do even if they wanted.

Miss Arlotta nodded, a sadness crossing her face. Then she straightened, all business again. "Which brings me to another point. Your couple hadn't yet crossed the threshold when Daphne spied you, *fully* materialized, sitting in the bay window, drinking from your flask. Make that three black marks."

"*Three?!*" Belle jerked her gaze to the judge. "Do you hear this? I'm being hornswoggled!"

He looked up, his blue eyes as sharp and clear as they'd been a hundred and nine years ago. "Belle, Miss Arlotta has used sound judgment in her decision making. If she says three, then three it is."

Belle stared out the window at birds circling lazily in the blue sky. The vast, endless blue sky. With a weighty sigh, she looked back at Miss Arlotta. "Two. That was your original offer."

A small smile creased Miss Arlotta's red lips. "Two it is, then."

Despite her mood, Belle had to smile, too. So this is what Miss Arlotta had wanted all along—Belle's buy-in' that two black marks was fair. The lady was one savvy negotiator.

"Always love doin' business with you, darlin'," Miss Arlotta said, floating past and touching Belle's long auburn hair. "Now, get back down there and heat things up some more for those two. Because if you succeed in helping two *strangers* see the light and fall in love, well, I think that'd be worth a bonus gold star, don't you?"

Bonus gold star? That could wipe out two black marks in a heartbeat.

"I'll see you one, and raise you one for *two* bonus gold stars," countered Belle, accepting the challenge.

She floated out of the room, catching a congratulatory smile from the judge on her way out.

ANDY HELD Daphne's hand, not liking the feel of that heavy, cold ring on her finger. Her engagement ring. *What in the hell am I doing? She's getting hitched to another guy.*

Andy led her to the love seat and gestured for her to sit down. "Take a load off and I'll bring you a slice."

Take a load off. He fought the urge to roll his eyes at himself. Words he'd say to a buddy, not a lovely lady with whom he'd just shared one hot moment. Nothing had been said, not out loud anyway, but the way she'd looked at him had damn near brought him to his knees.

He looked at her sitting on the love seat, the last light of day casting her in a hazy glow. Her eyes were soft, dreamy-like, so unlike those flashing eyes that had first met his in the lobby. *Not such a tough cookie, although she sure can put on a good show.* He thought back to his granddad saying, ''The hardest shell protects the softest heart,'' and for the first time, Andy knew exactly what the old man meant.

Her jean jacket was slightly open and he couldn't help but look at a delectable patch of skin on her neck, creamy and golden in the ebbing sunlight. The way a lock of dark hair curled seductively against her cheek. He'd been so close to her just moments ago...so close he'd felt her warmth, smelled her rose-scented perfume. What had it been called? Oh yeah, Dulcinea.

Dulcinea. The woman whose hidden beauty, indeed her very heart, moved Don Quixote to become a heroic knight.

''Bring me?'' she said.

''What?''

''You said you'd bring me a slice.''

''Yes...'' For an instant, no more, he allowed himself to fantasize what it'd be like to press his lips to that creamy spot of skin, to lick and taste her...

''Where are you eating?''

Reel it in, buddy. He dragged his gaze back to her eyes. ''Over there,'' he said hoarsely. Belatedly, he gestured toward the far table.

''Why?''

Because that far away, I won't be tempted to touch you. ''Because the love seat isn't big enough for the two of us.''

''What?''

He raked a hand through his hair, feeling its dampness at the hairline. Screw explaining what the hell he thought he was doing eating all the way across the room. He could be halfway across the world and be gorged with need for her. He wanted to tell her as much, open the floodgates and confess the effect she had on him, but the cost was too high. He couldn't play at love with her and hope to win.

Not with a damn Remington.

He glanced at the sheet dividing the bed.

"You're one to question seating arrangements." He hated the shift in his tone. He was wracked with guilt and desire and it shot out his mouth with a cocksure defensiveness like a downhill train with no brakes.

Somewhere along the way, he'd lost his sweet-talkin' edge. But it was all that stood between him and sure disaster.

"*You* put up a sheet to define some frickin' demarcation line," he barked, pacing away from her. "What're you going to do if I accidentally slip over the line? Call the bed police?"

She blinked rapidly. "What are you so angry about?"

He glared at her ring, then looked at her jean jacket. It was comfortably warm in the room, no need for Daphne to still wear it.

Screw the jacket.

He didn't get why she was wearing that damn ring.

He turned and headed back to the table, wishing to hell this weekend was already over.

5

DAPHNE MOVED to the bay window and looked down at the small town of Maiden Falls. The streetlamps were coming on, the drops of light illuminating people scurrying into restaurants and shops. Others were bundled up in their coats, heads bowed against the evening mountain chill. In Denver, it might be warm enough to sit at outdoor cafés, but springtime crept a little more slowly into the mountains.

Daphne spied a girl flipping a Closed sign in the window of a hair salon, housed on the first floor of a colorful Victorian building. It might be 2004, but Maiden Falls still had that bygone allure. A picturesque haven. No wonder this honeymoon hotel was so popular.

When she had jumped on that tour bus, Daphne had thought Maiden Falls would be the perfect haven for her, too. Away from all her worries in the big city, a place where she could be anonymous and free and kick up her Prada heels one last time. And she'd fulfilled part of that—she *was* free of the judgments of her family, Gordo and all the prying eyes and whispered asides.

But now she realized she hadn't run away from but

to something. And facing it was far more difficult than what she'd left behind.

Because, away from all those big-city critics, she was forced to face her toughest one. Herself. Forced to face her deepest needs and fears. Her need to please her family and Gordo. Her fear of not being correct, conventional enough. Bottom line, her desperation to be something she wasn't.

Funny how some time alone could raise one's self-doubts. *No wonder people rushed about, throwing all their energy into battling external problems. Easier to fix something like a broken car than look inside and fix a broken dream.*

Easier to say "I do" than "I can't."

She looked at her ring, which felt big and heavy and cold. Marrying Gordo was a reaction to her family, to that damn *Denver Post* article, to everyone who had ever called her the black sheep of the prestigious Remington dynasty.

But trying to fit her life into Gordo's was a death knell for her spirit. Sure, she'd get that hefty trust fund on her wedding day—something her parents dangled in front of her like a platinum-coated carrot—but it had all kinds of unspoken conditions tied to it. Foremost, that she never do anything to embarrass Gordo or her family. Her very being was to be bleached and washed and cleansed until there was no Daphne left.

Like a ghost.

She toyed with the ring, turning it slightly on her finger, realizing it'd grown looser the past day or so.

Belle floated through the door, saw Andy and Daphne's chilly standoff and halted.

Dang, darn and double tarnation!

With a huff, she pulled out her whiskey flask and took a swig. *If somebody had told me I'd spend my afterlife helping mortals find true love to redeem myself for all the love I faked, I would have been a schoolmarm instead of a working girl.*

She took another swig, then corked the flask while staring at Andy fussin' over the table and Daphne starin' out the window.

Too much fussin' and starin' and way too much space between these two.

Belle glanced up at the chandelier. She'd never understood why these current-day types liked bringing the sun inside. Gas lights and candlelight were always so much more romantic...

Hmm. She glanced at the candle on the marble table, back to the chandelier. She needed some ghostly help on this one. *Time to get Rosebud's nose out of a book and get her to do a little "adjustment" on the electric-ality in my room.*

Belle floated back out through the door.

A few moments later, the lights went out.

"What the hell?" muttered Andy. "Looks like a power failure."

"Maybe we should call the front desk."

"Sure, let me get to the phone." He paused, muttered an expletive. "Or maybe we should wait it out. I don't want people roaming about in here. I promised you anonymity."

She smiled to herself, thinking how Gordo would have scoffed if she'd begged for a reprieve from the spotlight. Funny how Andy, with his rough-and-tumble appearance, was actually more sensitive to her wishes.

Sensitive...and protective.

"Maybe it's just the chandelier?" questioned Daphne. "If the lights work in the bathroom, I can hide in the tub or something while they check things in the bedroom."

She sidled to the bathroom, fumbled for the switch. A cold chill skittered past, raising goose bumps on her arms. "Keep the window closed. It's cold out."

"Window *is* closed," called out Andy from the other room.

The chill passed, but her goose bumps stayed. Giving herself a mental shake, she flipped the switch. "Lights are off in here, too."

"Then it's definitely a power fail—" Andy paused. "Forget that theory. Light's spilling from the hallway underneath the door."

After a long moment of silence, punctuated by a sharp whistle of wind outside the window, Daphne spoke up. "Isn't there a candle on the table?"

Fumbling sounds. "Yes. A big one, too, so it should throw off some light."

"Got a match?"

"Not since Sting."

"Very funny. Let's light the candle and wait it out. We're probably not the only room affected. They'll fix the source of the problem, and no one will be the wiser that I'm here."

A moment later, a candle flickered, casting a golden haze over the table. Shaking out the match, Andy said, "Got fresh batteries in my CD player. Pizza's still warm. I say it's time to party."

"Got any decent CDs?" she teased, feeling lighter now that the tension had lifted. She headed toward the table.

He snorted. "Oh ye of little faith. I brought Widespread Panic, Allman Brothers, vintage Led Zeppelin—"

"Jalapeños and hard rock. Hope they have Tums in the minibar."

"Ah! The minibar! I like how you think, dear lady. Critical that we salvage some of its finer *accoutrements*. Wouldn't want things to spoil with the electricity off." He picked up the candle and headed to the armoire, which housed the compact refrigerator.

"Hotels don't put perishable items in minibars," Daphne said, taking a seat at the table.

"I beg to differ." The compact refrigerator door squeaked open. Let's see...a half bottle of Buena Vista merlot. Some fancy French-sounding chardonnay. Ah, little airplane bottles of whiskey and vodka. Yes, those would *definitely* spoil. Let me grab a few. Wine for the lady?"

Daphne had to smile. Gordo would have been fussing and fuming under similar circumstances, but Andy made this an adventure.

"I'll take the merlot. It goes well with meat."

"We're eating pizza."

"From the sounds of what you ordered, it sounded like meat on a cheesy crust."

He laughed. A hearty, boisterous sound. "I know you're a princess, but please don't tell me this is your first pizza."

"Very funny."

"What's your favorite kind?"

She thought a moment. "Goat cheese and porcini mushroom."

"Just what I thought. It's your first pizza." Carrying little bottles in one hand, the candle in the other, he headed back to the table, "To show you I have a sensitive side, I have Dido's latest single. Record companies, among others, are always mailing freebies to the *Post*."

"Dido?"

He stopped, stared at her. "Miss Remington, I do believe you've led a sheltered life. Come, let me teach you a few things."

A shiver of excitement raced down her spine. She was starting to feel like the old Daphne, rebellious and ready for adventure. It felt great to shed the Stepford Socialite she'd become, always trying so damn hard to fit in, not cause waves. To hell with that woman. Daphne wanted all the things she'd come here for, excitement and adventure, and she yearned to discover those things, and more, with this man.

In the dark, she eased off the ring. And as she dropped it into her jacket pocket, a weight lifted off her heart.

A minute later, she and Andy were eating pizza, listening to a honey-voiced woman—Dido—and sipping whiskey. Yes, whiskey. When Andy teased her about merlot with meat, Daphne decided to surprise him, drink what he was drinking. It'd been worth the double take he'd given her.

Andy sang a few words of the song, harmonizing with Dido.

"You have a nice voice."

"My granddad put me in a boys' choir."

"Get out." She took a sip of whiskey, wincing at its sting.

"You sure you don't want merlot?"

She blinked and swallowed, the alcohol burning a path all the way to her toes. "No," she rasped.

"Don't tell me this is your first whiskey, too?"

She cleared her throat. "I had a mint julep in New Orleans."

"It's your first." He helped himself to another slice. "So, tell me about this boys' choir."

"I kicked and yelled, picked a few fights. That first year I lived with my granddad, seemed I had a perpetual black eye. Then, one day I realized I dug being in the choir. Belting out tunes, being part of something bigger than my problems. It was cool."

"Bigger than your problems...?" The music ended, emphasizing her question. His eyes narrowed speculatively and Daphne regretted her inquisitiveness.

He doesn't know whether to trust me.

His gaze wandered around the room's shadows. "My mom was a drug addict," he finally said, his gaze returning to Daphne's. "Child services stepped in, removed me from our home. My granddad was the only relative who wanted me, so..." He shrugged, took a drink.

He trusts me. A warmth flowed through her. "So, he inherited one angry kid."

Andy nodded. "Angry enough for two kids, he used to say. I look back now and marvel how the old man loved me in spite of myself. They broke the mold when they made him."

Andy's eyes glistened, and she thought for a moment he wanted to say something else, but he didn't. The only sound in the stretched-out silence was the faintest trickle, the first drops of thawed water in the falls, broken only by the hoot of an owl.

Andy suddenly pushed the pizza box aside. "Enough about me. I'll lug my laptop over here and interview you while you finish."

She'd gotten too close to his pain, secrets that ran deep. She could still see that chip-on-the-shoulder kid. Saw it in Andy's swagger, his cocksure ways. But tonight she'd also seen the kid whose life had been shattered and the man who'd evolved from that pain. Stronger, she'd guess, in the broken places.

But even so, she wanted to protect those places in him, just as he'd been protective of her.

"Okay," she said. "Let's interview me."

OVER AN HOUR later, Andy was typing at the keyboard. Scattered on the table were four empty airplane bottles and a nearly finished half bottle of merlot only because Daphne had teased him about never trying it before, saying if she was going to have a "first" then so should he.

He'd always been a sucker for a dare.

Especially from a beautiful woman whose eyes sparkled in the candlelight. And who had a wickedly seductive little habit of touching her tongue to her lip while thinking.

He liked making her think.

"So," Andy said, reading his computer screen, "you were trundled off to boarding school in England—how Harry Potter—when you were twelve. Hated the teachers. Hated the outfits." He paused, looked at Daphne. "Anything you liked?"

She touched her tongue to her lip.

His heart thudded dully. He eased out a long, pent-up breath and dropped his gaze.

Bad move.

She sat with one heel pulled in close to her butt on the chair. Candlelight flickered provocatively along her cargo pants and bare, shapely calf. While she thought, she wriggled her naked toes. Her red-dipped, begging-to-be-sucked toes.

"You're not going to write about *all* of this, right?"

"Why would I write about your toes?" he rasped.

"What?"

He jerked his gaze back to her face. "Your foes," he said quickly. He cleared his throat, hunched over the keyboard. "You're the one who said you hated the teachers, right? Well, maybe you were more than a little irritating to them, too."

"I beg your pardon—"

"No, I'm not using everything. This is part of my data-gathering before I draft the article. I like to know the whole shebang, then I whittle it down. And, as I promised, you'll approve the final story before it's printed."

Raking his hand through his hair, he stared intently at the computer screen. "So, where were we? Okay, what did you like at the boarding school?"

She was quiet for so long, he had to look over at her again.

She'd stuck the tip of her pinkie into one of the little bottles and was waggling it back and forth. "I liked a hole in the fence."

A lesser man would have jumped her right then. Or imploded, pieces of him strewn from coast to coast.

"At boarding school," she continued. Waggle waggle. "I discovered this hole in the fence surrounding the property and I loved sneaking through it and running barefoot through the nearby field."

An image of Daphne naked, running in moonlight filled his mind. "Streaking?"

"What?"

"Uh, you ran barefoot." In his mind's eye, the naked Daphne turned and looked at him over her shoulder, laughing for him to follow. "Renegade Remington even at an early age, eh?" he croaked.

"I've got an idea."

"Yeah, so do I, but let's not share, okay?" He gently took the bottle off her finger before she whacked it against something. The last thing he needed was a trip to the emergency room where he'd have to explain why and how G. D. McCormick's fiancée, who just happened to be sharing his room at a honeymoon hotel, got glass shards in her pinkie.

Her very soft and deliciously small pinkie.

"You're sweet," she murmured.

He held her hand, too aware of the heat of her skin against his. "Just taking care of you."

"A real gentleman."

"Keep that thought." Words more for him than her. *Keep it together, keep your cool.* He released her hand, gathered the rest of the airplane bottles.

"Did you play an instrument as a kid?" he asked, all business again. He set the bottles in a nearby trash can that held the folded-up pizza box. "Any hobbies?"

"Yes." She straightened. Sort of. More like, she raised up and leaned over in a teetering sort of way. "Is it warm in here?"

It's a frickin' inferno. "Tell me about your hobby."

She flapped open her jacket. "Why don't you check the thermostat? Maybe it got pushed up again."

He glanced at her breasts pressing against the silky green. *I'm a dead man if she takes off her jacket.* He got up, taking the candle with him, and checked the thermostat. "Not even seventy," he announced. "You're hot because you've been drinking."

"And you're not?"

"Not what?"

"Hot?"

Maybe he should do the rest of the interview over here across the room, away from green silk and wayward pinkies. "No."

"Liar."

"Okay, yes." Another image of Daphne flashed through his mind. Naked again. In bed. *This* bed. With him. No hanging demarcation sheet, no barriers, just two bodies moving against each other in warm, liquid movements.

He stifled a groan.

"Something wrong?"

He took a deep breath, blew it out and headed back to the table. "No." He sat down. "Hobby?"

She blinked, her eyes wide. "You mad at me?"

"No." He placed his fingers on home row—a good place for them to be. "Hobby?"

She put her elbow on the table and rested her chin in her hand. Her eyes were soft, the color of mink in the candlelight. "Photography."

"Pictures of fellow socialites, ballroom dancing lessons, what?"

She arched a perfectly shaped eyebrow. "Okay,

you're not mad, but you're definitely being testy. Fellow socialites? Ballroom dancing? I thought we toasted to not judging books by their covers."

Her jacket hung off one shoulder, exposing a lovely vision of skin against green silk.

"My apologies," he whispered, feeling like the sorriest guy who'd ever walked the planet. Alone in a hotel room with a beautiful babe who was too hot. Forget a bunch of pissed-off Remingtons and one gubernatorial candidate. One wrong move and Andy would lose the story, lose the opportunity to write the book of his dreams. That's what this was all about.

Wasn't it?

"Tell me about your photography," he said in his deepest, sincerest, un-sweet-talkin'-est voice.

She scanned his face. Seemingly pleased that he was indeed being sincere, she smiled. "Easier to see. Let's plug the phone line into your laptop, check out some of my photos on a Web site."

A few minutes later, he'd opened a browser window. "Web site name?"

"Mrs. Allen's Halfway House."

"You're kidding."

"No, I'm serious." She absentmindedly played with a button on her jacket. "Allen. A-l-l-e-n."

"Never would have guessed," he mumbled, typing it in.

A window opened with a picture of a Queen Anne building on a tree-lined street. Underneath it were the words "Welcome to Mrs. Allen's Halfway House."

"You took the picture of the house?" he asked.

Daphne scooted her chair closer and peered at the screen. "No, they've had that forever. See the links on the left side? Click on Success Stories."

He did.

A list of women's first names was displayed, with the notation that the names had been changed to protect the women's anonymity.

"Click on one of those," said Daphne. She gestured to the links, her arm brushing against his. Fire blazed across his skin.

With great effort, he clicked on Amanda. A picture displayed. A young woman with flyaway blond hair and pink-flushed cheeks, but her eyes said it all. Dark pools of hurt, wiser than her years.

"You took this photo?" Andy asked.

"Yes."

"She's like an old soul in a young body."

"So true." Daphne leaned closer to the screen, the glow highlighting her delicate features. "Amanda started using drugs when she was twelve, was married with a baby at seventeen. By nineteen, she'd lost her marriage, her child and couldn't hold down a job because of her addiction. After rehab, Amanda stayed at Mrs. Allen's during her reentry into the real world. That's when I met her. I took her picture as a gift to her child—she was fighting for her parental rights at the time and was terrified she'd lose. Good news is, she now shares custody with her ex."

"Definitely a success story," Andy murmured, trying to assimilate the pieces of this surprising story. Not Amanda's, but Daphne's. "How'd you end up doing this?"

"The photos?"

"The halfway house, the women..." He clicked on another link, looked at a photograph of a tired-looking middle-aged woman smoking a cigarette. Through a plume of smoke, one caught a slight, mischievous smile. "These portraits are amazing."

"Thank you. I attended Brooks Institute, in Santa Barbara, for a few years after college, but my family never seemed all that interested in my 'hobby' of photography. During a fundraiser for Mrs. Allen's Halfway House a few years ago, one of the girls saw me with my camera and asked if I'd take a picture of her for her family. That led to other requests from the women, which eventually led to some of my photos being displayed on their walls."

"And on their Web site."

"Yes. The women whose success stories are on the site speak openly of their recovery, and approved their photos being used, but their anonymity is maintained."

Andy looked at Daphne. "Still waters run deep."

She paused. "Or maybe you misjudged my cover."

"How come people don't know this side of you?"

"Uh, maybe because the *Post* prefers sensationalist news when it comes to the Remingtons?"

"Touché." Andy stared at the picture for a long moment, wishing his own mother had received help, had lived in such a place. "I'm very impressed." He didn't trust himself to say more. Andy Branigan, who could sweet-talk the birds out of the trees—or so his grand-dad swore—didn't trust himself to express what he was feeling.

How deeply Daphne was affecting him.

"Why haven't you done something with your pho-tography?"

"Like show it at a gallery?" Daphne shrugged. "I didn't think, outside of Mrs. Allen's, that anyone would be interested."

It hit Andy, the irony of a woman like Daphne using her pictures to help build other women's self-esteem, but not her own.

"There's another photo I'd like to show you," Daphne said. "Do you mind?" She inched closer, her hands poised to take over the keyboard.

"Be my guest," Andy said, leaning back, liking her nearness. The candlelight cast a golden sheen on her silhouette, threading her dark curls with gold. And her scent, ah, that delicious scent. He took a stealthy lungful of Dulcinea.

"I keep this photo on my own Web site." On the screen was a grainy black-and-white photo of a man dressed in jeans held up by suspenders over a dark work shirt. Behind him were several women dressed in ill-fitting jackets, skirts and boots. One held a baby.

"My great-great-great-great-granddad Charlie," Daphne explained. "This was taken in 1893, right be-fore he struck gold. Family lore quotes him as saying

his happiest days were when he was a poor, struggling miner." She smiled to herself. "This photo was
taken during those days."

"Who are the women?" Andy asked

"Let's see..." Daphne touched her tongue to her
bottom lip. "The woman to his right was his recently
wed bride, my great-great-great-great-grandmother
Sarah. The other woman, Elizabeth or Betsy—her last
name is lost—was a neighbor who, after he struck it
rich, became their housekeeper. The little girl is hers,
named Jo."

The decanter rattled.

Andy looked at it, then Daphne. Together they both
whispered, "Wind" then smiled. Crazy decanter.
Whatever rocked its world seemed to be rocking
theirs, too.

Andy stared for a long moment at Daphne. She was
a damn attractive woman, but tonight he saw more.
He saw the integrity behind her beauty.

A sensual smile curved her face. God, he loved her
smile. Loved that she was doing it more, too.

"You," she whispered.

"What about me?"

"I like you."

"If we hadn't emptied all the airplane bottles, I'd
say no more for you."

"Say it."

"What?"

"No more for me."

Andy steeled himself. Noble had never been his

calling card, but tonight he was playing it. Had to, even though his every nerve ending was on fire with pure, unadulterated desire for this woman.

"May I remind you that you're engaged."

"Enga*ging*?" Her mouth raised to his, the lips pink and full and oh so ready.

He could barely breathe for the ache she fired in him. "Engaged," he repeated. "As in almost married to G. D. McCormick."

She held up her hand. "No ring."

"You took it off."

She nodded.

"Does Mr. McCormick know?"

"Not yet."

"Then you're still engaged."

She leaned closer until her lips grazed his. Her ragged breaths were warm and whiskey-sweet.

"Tonight, I belong to no one, Andy, except you. Kiss me."

6

DAPHNE PULLED BACK slightly and looked at him through the dark fringe of her lashes. "Kiss me," she whispered again.

A gust of wind jangled the windows. The candle flame leapt.

"Not a good idea," Andy murmured. He stood up and pushed back his chair.

"Yes," Daphne whispered, standing, too. "Downright terrible."

"I don't, uh, want this."

"Yeah, me neither." And she gave him a look, the kind of look a woman gives a man she wants to wake up with. Sexy and playful and damn unrepentant...

And too damn hard to resist.

Andy lowered his lips, hesitated. A fleeting thought of resistance skittered through his mind, followed by a speck of rationalization it would only be a kiss...

Just a kiss...

His gaze trained on her mouth—that wicked, teasing mouth. A heavy pounding started in his chest, reverberated in his ears as he bent his head closer.

Just a kiss...

The moment his lips brushed against hers, Andy realized what a fool he'd been. There was nothing *just* about Renegade Remington, nothing *just* about the mouth that clung hungrily to his. Nothing rational about the fingers that tunneled into his hair. The room receded, taking with it any last shred of common sense he had.

Whatever stupid idea he'd had about only a kiss exploded, replaced by something wild and dangerous as his lips consumed hers, his tongue sliding into her wet, yielding mouth. He probed deeper, aching to taste her fully. She groaned deep in her throat and he tugged her closer, loving the feel of her breasts flattened against his chest and how her body molded to his.

Just a kiss?

The hot, moist taste of her was devastatingly female. Pungent with the sting of whiskey. His hands thrust into her hair—so soft, so silky—and he dragged his mouth up her cheek, nibbling, licking, stealing her sweetness until he buried his face in her hair, and inhaled its flowery fragrance as though he'd never taken a decent breath in his life.

"So...good," he murmured, pulling back to stare at her heavy-lidded eyes and reddened lips before claiming her mouth again with a deep, primal growl.

It went on and on—a minute, an hour, forever—until he withdrew his fingers from her hair and slid them slowly down the curves of her body until his hands rested on her hips.

He wanted her.

Desperately, madly.

Wanted to drag her to the bed, onto the love seat, hell, take her right here on the floor. Rip those pretty pants off and bury himself deep inside her.

With a shuddered groan, he tightened his hold on her hips, willing himself to rein it in, fighting sizzling images that blasted through his brain. The two of them in bed, naked. Her legs wrapped around his hips, Daphne crying out his name. Again and again and again.

The candle flame licked higher.

Then suddenly blew out.

They held each other in the dark for a long moment, their hearts pounding, their breaths coming hard.

"What happened?" she whispered.

"Candle went out."

"How?"

For a second he didn't respond. He rested his chin on her head and took a deep, calming breath. What had just transpired between them was dark, primordial and, oh God, the hottest thing he'd ever experienced.

"Don't know," he finally answered. Didn't want to know, either. He'd always been a black-and-white kinda guy, never buying into deeper meanings. Waste of time, he'd always thought. You live, you eat, you lust, you die.

Then his grandfather had died, ripping away the one thing that gave life meaning. Andy swore and fought with his grief, only to finally give up. He didn't have any answers, but he did have the old man's wisdom, encapsulated into anecdotes that offered some solace.

And Andy had continued to live, although life didn't really touch him as much.

Until now.

Something about being here, in this room and with this woman, was undermining some fundamental aspect of his otherwise predictable, ordinary life. Strange occurrences had come to pass that he couldn't always explain. Powerful feelings rocked his body and mind. If there was a God, he—or she—had grabbed Andy by the shoulders and given him a good shake.

He felt as though he were being reprimanded to look around, see things differently.

He didn't want that.

Did he?

On the table, something caught his eye.

"Daphne," he whispered, slowly turning her around.

"Oh my God." Her body stiffened. "How'd that get there?"

The laptop was where they'd left it on the table, but its screen had changed. Instead of the historical photograph, it now displayed an image of two cards, the King and Queen of Hearts.

Daphne laughed nervously. "You did that."

"No—"

"Yes, you did! You had to."

"We must have accidentally clicked on a link—"

"No, we didn't. That's a screen saver." She laughed again, a bit more relieved. "A romantic screen saver." She lowered her voice and turned to face Andy. The spare, hazy light from the computer screen and the moon through the bay window gave Daphne an almost ethereal glow.

"And you acted as though we shouldn't kiss," she said in a low voice. "Andy Branigan, you don't fool me. You're a mush."

"Sure," he murmured, suddenly wishing he'd really done something like that to please her. "Problem is, I don't have such a screen saver. No bookmarks to any card sites, either."

And he thought about saying more. How he didn't believe in things like ghosts or true love, but knew he'd be a liar because those beliefs were being sorely tested in this damn room.

Reel it in, focus on reality. Like his deadline. The interview. And that the lady—despite her persuasive "no ring, no ties" line—belonged to another man.

Time to take five.

"Let's go to bed," he said, easing away from Daphne.

"Now you're talking."

"*With* the sheet up."

"WHAT'S WRONG, Belle?" Sunshine hovered nearby on the roof, the layers of her white dress floating about her curvaceous form. "Not like you to get maudlin.

Heck, you're the eternal optimist, always advisin' us 'Never fold a good hand' even if you have to fake it if you're dealt a bad one. The girls giving you a bad time again about target practice?"

Belle snorted. "Like Flo and her persnickety self ever affected me." She took a long drag of her cigarillo and stared up at the moon. "No, it's 'cause I'm darn close to the Big Picnic and I got a couple in my room sleeping on opposite sides of the bed." There were other things—the baby in the photo—but Belle never talked about that part of her old life. Except to Miss Arlotta.

"Your specialty is planting thoughts in lovers' minds—already tried that?"

Belle nodded. "With those two, though, it's like takin' a horse to water who'll barely take a sip." She flashed a knowing look at Sunshine. "There's a little problem with the woman, Daphne, being betrothed to another, but I can *feel* her heart's wishes. She *belongs* with that man in my room, and he with her. But that ruffian has too many dang morals." Belle took another puff.

"I know you, Belle. You'll get that horse to drink," Sunshine said with a wink. "Then give 'em some of your best tips to spice things up. That'll cinch your last notch."

Belle nodded, looked out at the dark, heavy clouds hovering in the west. "Looks like another spring snowstorm rollin' in."

"Shame, too," said Sunshine. "The falls were just

Tell him. Before it's too late.

"Drake, we had a child." Her soul's secret, the one thing she'd always wished she'd shared with him. If life was about following your heart, she'd failed miserably.

His eyes glistened with emotion.

How long would he—could he—stay? She had to tell him what happened. Before it was too late.

"On the run after Tombstone, near Denver, I discovered I was with child. A local doctor knew a couple who desperately wanted children and could provide a real home."

Drake nodded, and for a moment, Belle wished he'd yell at her, blame her. Because it would hurt less than his tender, compassionate look.

"I only asked if they'd name her Jo."

Drake smiled. She did, too, knowing they were both remembering that summer he'd taught her to read by using the book *Little Women.*

"In '91, yellow fever swept through the area," she whispered. "A customer told me a couple in a nearby town had died. Them and their little girl, Jo."

Belle pursed her lips, her mind stumbling over the rest. How Miss Arlotta, the only one who knew Belle's story, had helped her through those grief-stricken months until she could work again.

"Oh my darlin' girl," murmured Drake, his form fading, "I wish you hadn't been alone."

She reached out her hand. "Don't leave—"

But her only answer was the whistling wind and the faint hush of the nearby falls.

"WHERE'S the baby?" A man's muscled arms, brown below rolled-up shirt sleeves, wrapped around Daphne's waist from behind.

"At the neighbor's," she answered, wiping the juice of apples off her hands onto a towel. She pushed aside a bowl filled with the peeled fruit.

"You smell sweet." He nuzzled her ear, his warm breath making her shiver. "Like hot apple pie."

A breeze flitted through the kitchen window, bringing scents of summer roses that mingled with the baking ham and buttermilk biscuits. The man turned her to face him.

It was Andy. And yet, at the same time, it wasn't. The shock of red hair, those piercing blue eyes were his. Even that cocksure smile. But different was the work shirt, soiled and stained from hard labor, pulled tight across his wide shoulders. And the sun-kissed brown of his skin, as though he spent most of his life outdoors.

Her heart pounded as he tugged her closer. He smelled of sun and sweat and man. He leaned down, rubbed his nose playfully against hers and murmured huskily, "Darlin' girl of mine."

It was again familiar and, at the same time, not. Daphne knew this teasing led to passion, just as she knew the ridges and muscles underneath his clothes, where to touch, how to please. How it felt to be beneath him when their bodies joined.

And yet, this room, this very world, felt surreal. Vaguely familiar, but if she thought about it enough, she knew she'd remember fully. Like a word on the tip of your tongue.

A grin sauntered across his lips, and he gave her *that* look—his blue eyes burning into hers, scorching her with their need—and suddenly it didn't matter what she'd thought was real or unreal as she let herself be swept away on a tide of feelings.

"I want you," he growled.

He touched her, oh so lightly stroking her cheek, the path of his roughened fingers leaving a tingling sensation that spread slowly, completely, throughout her body, leaving in its wake a physical craving that filled every cell of her being.

"Yes," she whispered.

Desire thickened the air. He cupped her cheek, angling her head as he kissed her long and hard. Tendrils of her hair lifted with another breeze, tickling and teasing her skin. She groaned, opened her mouth wider, tangled her tongue with his.

He trailed his hand down her cotton bodice, the heat of his fingers seeping through the fabric to her hardened nipples. A heaviness flooded the aching hollow between her legs.

"Yes," she whispered again. "Oh, yes…"

Up came her skirt. His hand grazed her thigh, slipped into her drawers. Hot, skilled fingers touched her and she arched her back, panting as another breeze rushed over her moistened face.

"I...need...you," he whispered huskily.

With anxious persistence he tugged her forward. She eagerly complied. Her breath quickening with his, she spread her legs, ready to succumb to the sweetly wicked heat....

Knock knock knock.

Andy faded, the kitchen faded....

Knock knock knock.

Daphne blinked open her eyes, looking foggily around the room. Brass four-poster bed. Chandelier. Familiar...and yet...

She wriggled her toes under the cream-colored satin bedspread and stared at the sunlight filtering through gauzy curtains fringing a bay window. It was all coming back to her...the room, Maiden Falls...

Knock knock knock.

She glanced down at a man's bare arm, dusted with golden-red hair, thrust over her naked chest.

Ohhhh...

That was coming back to her, too. Last night. Little airplane bottles of whiskey. That kiss...

Oh, God, that kiss.

But...

She frowned, jerked her gaze up to the track lights on the ceiling over the bed. *Where's the sheet?* She glanced back at her naked breasts—covered by that very naked, very male arm—again. *Didn't he loan me one of his T-shirts to wear?*

Knock knock knock.

Andy groaned, snuggled closer. "Darlin' girl," he mumbled.

Darlin' girl. That's what the man—Andy?—called me in the dream.

Daphne slid out of bed, the cool air assaulting every spot of her naked body, trying her best to remember when she'd doffed—or Andy had removed?—the bright orange Tony Stewart NASCAR T-shirt he'd given her to sleep in. She remembered slipping it on...but didn't remember much after that.

Knock knock knock.

"Coming!" she called out. She trotted to the bathroom and grabbed a hotel robe—fluffy, white—off a hook, then headed to the door. After peering through the peephole, she opened the door slightly and looked at the bellhop, the kid with the braces, who gave her a quick down-up glance.

"Sorry to, uh, wake you."

"It's all right." She looked around for a cart. "Did you bring coffee?"

"No, but they have courtesy coffee and rolls downstairs." He handed her a paper. "Brought you a fax."

"Fax?"

The kid nodded, his eyes darting past her to the bed, back to her. "From the *Denver Post* with instructions to be delivered immediately to a Mr. Andrew Branigan. We tried phoning your room, couldn't get through, so I'm hand-delivering it."

"Right," she murmured, remembering Andy hook-ing up the phone line to his computer last night. They'd forgotten to reconnect it. "Thanks." She accepted the paper. "Let me get some change—"

She glanced back at the room, wondering where she'd put her purse, half expecting to see a pile of ripped orange T-shirt lying somewhere.

"Uh, no problem," the boy said. "After all, I interrupted you two—" His cheeks flushed. With an awkward wave, he suddenly turned and left.

She shut the door, wondering if last night she and Andy really had... No, no way. She'd know. A few bitty bottles of whiskey wasn't enough to do her in, wipe out her memory.

Because she well remembered *wanting* to do what she *hadn't* done. In fact, she'd been pretty darn desperate to do what she didn't get to do. Jeez. Now that she thought back to last night, she cringed at her "kiss me" demand.

Demand? More like begging.

Daphne Remington had never *begged* a man for it.

She stared at Andy, lying in the bed.

That's how he looked in the hot images that had filled her mind last night. It was as though somebody had taken over her thoughts, zapping her brain with hot, sizzling pictures of a scrumptiously naked Andy making burn-down-the-house love to her.

She closed her eyes. *Oh God. I begged.*

"Who was that at the door?"

She opened her eyes. Andy, the sheet hanging dangerously low on his hips, glanced sleepily at her.

"Bellboy," she croaked. "You got a fax." *And by the way, I'm not the begging type. Really.*

Andy propped himself up on his elbow, blinked lazily. "Has to be from Frank, my features editor. That man's tracking instincts could shame a bloodhound." Yawning, he waggled his fingers for the paper.

Daphne handed it to him, remembering the dream. In it, Andy's body had been more sunburned. A ruddy brown that emanated heat. And although she didn't get to see him naked in the dream, she'd *known* what he looked like and it was pretty darn near what she saw now. Muscled chest carpeted with wild swirls of golden-red chest hair. Strong shoulders. And those hands. Brown...big...

"You can let go."

"Sorry." She released her grip on the fax.

He shot a crooked grin at her. "Too much lovin' in the kitchen, eh?"

Daphne did a double take. "What?"

"Hmm?" He gave his head a shake, yawned again. "Sorry, my mind's playing tricks on me...started dipping back into my dream last night..."

"Kitchen?"

He cocked her a sleepy grin. "Yeah, there was a kitchen."

"That...that was in my dream, too. We were in it...we lived there..." Heat raced to her face as she remembered the rest. Did he also experience *that*?

His smile slowly dissolved, replaced by a perplexed look. He checked out Daphne's robe, the bed, the room as though finally realizing just where they were, too.

He looked back at her. "Daphne," he said huskily, "we had the same dream."

The glass decanter on the table rattled.

7

ANDY LOOKED from the decanter back to Daphne. "That's not the wind."

Daphne shook her head no, her eyes wide.

"Think somebody is trying to tell us something?"

"Like—" she looked around "—like who-whoever blew out the candle last night?"

He cocked an eyebrow. "I thought that was you."

"Me?" She snorted, gestured toward the spot where they'd stood last night. "How? Your body was between me and the candle! Not just between, but *against* me. *Hard.*" She skimmed her fingers down the front of her robe, scanning the covers over his body before returning her gaze to his.

"Baby, I was kidding." *But if you keep looking at me with that dewy-eyed what's-under-the-covers expression, I'm going to stop joking and get serious, fast.* Andy Branigan, known for his sweet-talkin' ways, was having one hell of a time keeping his lips under lock and key with this lady.

Nodding, she tugged on a curl. "Right," she whispered. "You were kidding." She suddenly grew preoccupied fussing with the sash on her robe. Without raising her gaze, she murmured, "And, uh, for the record, I wasn't begging."

"Excuse me?"

She looked up, all innocence. "Nothing."

"Beg?"

She shrugged, her face flushing.

"Ohh..." He absently stroked a spot on the bedspread. "You mean, when you said 'kiss me'?"

Damn if her cheeks didn't flame redder.

"I need to get dressed." Head high, she started making a beeline to the bathroom, where she'd changed her clothes last night.

"I'm not sure I'd call that *begging*," he called out after her. "*Worked up*, maybe. Or hot to trot—"

She came to a dead stop in front of the bathroom door, her back to him. "Seems to me you were 'hot to trot' yourself."

"I was." His gaze traveled down her body, stopping where the robe clung seductively to a rounded hip. "Still am," he said huskily. And for a moment, he was sucked into the fantasy of being in this room, a man and a woman, no rules.

But only for a moment.

He raked his hand through his hair, as though he could wipe away the knowledge of G. D. McCormick, what Daphne's life was outside of this room, this town. Maybe at this very moment they were stripped down to their bare selves—equals under the skin, so to speak—but that didn't change the fact that they came

from two different worlds. His rough and earthy, h.
sophisticated and privileged.

Even if she were single and free to choose whom-
ever she wanted to be with, would it be Andy? Would
she find him embarrassing, inadequate out in that upper-crust world where the air was thinner, the expectations higher?

Which was a big reason he kept pulling away. Oh,
he'd succumbed to the heat, all right—last night's kiss,
he'd been like a damn moth drawn to a bonfire—but
after a taste of the sweetest sin this side of heaven,
he'd backpedaled like some kind of Boy Scout. He'd
never been a push-pull kinda guy. A game player.
And if he was willing to own up to his damn insecu-
rity, he'd tell her why. Tell her he didn't enjoy this cat-
and-mouse game. Hell, he didn't get the nickname
"tomcat" by playing the mouse.

In the silence, he listened to the steady trickling of
the distant falls, the melting water like a whisper underneath the ice. Like last night's dream, a hazy image
of him and Daphne floating beneath his conscious-
ness...

That dream...

He closed his eyes, feeling the heated breezes caressing his skin, smelling the tart sweetness of apples.
Her hair had been longer, the loose tendrils tickling
his cheek when he'd kissed her. Her clothes—cotton
blouse and long, heavy skirt—seemed to be from another century. As though she were Daphne, yet
not her.

he opened his eyes.

She'd turned around, her dark hazel eyes piercing the distance between them. Her expression serious despite a telltale flush still suffusing her cheeks. But even with her somber mood, she looked like an angel wrapped in that cloud-like robe, the way her curly hair framed her face like a dark halo, the way the sunshine pouring through the window cast her in a golden light.

"God," he whispered, "you're beautiful."

He quickly dipped his head and scanned the fax. This was all becoming too *out there*. A dream of a place where they somehow belonged and loved. Being in this room where they belonged...and shouldn't love.

"Looks like Frank wants me to check out another honeymoon hotel after I leave here," he said nonchalantly, reading the fax. "Also wants me to call, discuss some things." He looked up at Daphne. "I'll need to do a bit of research in the inn today—"

"I don't want to be left alone."

At the paper, he'd often written that someone's eyes were large as saucers, one of those terms he overused to snag a quick image, but he'd never actually witnessed it before this moment. But considering what had gone on in here—rattling decanters, candles mysteriously blowing out, a strangely shared dream—he didn't blame Daphne for being frightened.

More than ever, he wanted to protect her. Take care of her.

"You know," he said, matter-of-factly, tossing the

fax aside. "I can write these fluff pieces in my sleep. I'll do a walk-around later, interview a few people, read brochures. I'll call Frank, tell him the article's coming together—"

"He doesn't know about me, right?"

"God, no. I mentioned I was drafting an idea for an interview because he reviews my uploaded articles on the server. This way, when he sees several files dated this weekend, he'll know to only check the one named honeymoon."

She nodded, her face softening into a smile, and he thought how she hadn't done that very often when they'd first met. Because of that, he cherished all the more the one she was bestowing on him at the moment. Wanted to give her more reasons to smile.

"Let's do something special," he suddenly said.

She arched a questioning eyebrow.

"Let's blow this popsicle stand and take in some fresh Colorado air." The idea came to him out of the blue, but now that he'd said it, it sounded perfect. A chance to stretch their legs, explore the rugged beauty of the region.

"I'd like that very much." She paused, bit her lip. "But, if someone recognizes me—I mean, not outdoors of course, but leaving the hotel. It's Sunday and this place is a mecca for brunches, weddings. People drive miles and miles for the inn's eggs Benedict."

"For some eggs and sauce?" He shook his head. "I know dives in Denver whose huevos rancheros could make a sinner a saint." He glanced at her leather purse. "Got sunglasses in that piece of luggage?"

"Yes."

"And I got a baseball cap." He doubled up a king size pillow and pushed it against the headboard. "Did a piece on robbers once. Did you know sunglasses and baseball caps are their favorite hold-up disguise?" He leaned back against the pillow. "Security cameras can't see their faces. Amazingly enough, even the very people they rob—who meet them right at eye level—have a hell of a time IDing the person."

"So, we're pulling a Bonnie and Clyde?" she teased.

"Hey, you're the one who came up here for a weekend of adventure and fun."

"I have a feeling life is like that with you any day of the week."

"Would you like that?" *A life with me every day of the week?*

As soon as he said the words, he regretted them.

A damn slip of the tongue because, of course, whatever was going on between them wasn't like *that*. And even if he was fool enough to think this was more than lust, people from different sides of the tracks weren't destined for the long haul. Shakespeare nailed that one with *Romeo and Juliet*.

An image of the old photograph suddenly flashed in Andy's mind, overriding his thoughts. He saw it as clearly as if it were before him now. The shanty, the man in the suspenders, the woman and the baby Jo...

"I have an idea," Andy said, breaking the silence.

"Let's visit your great-great—however many greats—granddad Charlie's place."

· "Know what?" Daphne played one bare foot along the hardwood floor. "I had that *exact* same thought riding up here on the bus. It's been years since I visited the place—time to reacquaint myself with some family history."

"Same ideas, same dreams. Maybe it's nothing weird, we're just two minds who think alike." Not that he bought into that one hundred percent, but he wanted to reassure Daphne. "Plus, speaking of adventures, I think you need to experience a joy ride in my fifteen-year-old Jeep."

She arched an eyebrow. *"Fifteen?"*

"Think of it as a finely aged merlot," he said with a wink, then glanced at the window. "Looks sunny, but April in the mountains can get iffy—definitely too cool to wear that piece of silk you call a top. I brought some flannel shirts, extra T's."

She glanced around the room, a perplexed look on her face.

"The Tony Stewart T-shirt is under the covers, wadded up by my feet."

"How did it get there?"

"You took it off." He scratched the stubble on his chin. "Right after you begged."

"I didn't beg—" She caught his look, realized he was kidding her. "Well," she continued, her tone lighter, "if I did, sure didn't get me far, did it?"

She opened the bathroom door and stepped inside.

But before she closed it, she looked at him over her shoulder and a teasing glint came into her eyes. "For the record, I'd like that."

"What?"

"A life with you, every day of the week."

After she shut the door, Andy blew out a low, pent-up whistle. Women like this could teach the tomcats of the world a thing or two about the game of cat-and-mouse.

"SO MANY people," murmured Daphne under her breath, skimming her fingers along the smooth wooden banister as she and Andy walked down the main staircase.

Below them, the lobby was a swarm of people dressed in their Sunday finest. With the winter off-season over, people were flocking to the historic inn for everything from a great meal to a wedding. Through the doors of the Golden Rule, the renowned restaurant, trills from a string quartet floated out into the lobby, mixing with people's chatter and laughter.

"Don't worry," Andy said, "you're incognito."

"I'm wearing lime-green Prada heels, cargo pants, a flaming red-and-gray flannel shirt over a tie-dyed shirt," Daphne said tightly. "I'm not incognito. I'm a walking emergency flare."

Andy pressed a reassuring hand on her back. "Yeah, but a very cute flare."

They reached the bottom of the stairs and stopped. She lowered her head to look at him over the top of her sunglasses, the bill of the baseball cap cutting off the top of his head.

"You pick the oddest times to sweet-talk me."

He cocked her a half grin. "Like to keep you on your toes."

"Oh, that you do, Mr. Branigan. Indeed you do."

They looked around the lobby. The room was a mix of upscale design with touches of the hotel's bygone grandeur in an occasional red velvet settee or the potted palms in their brass pots.

"There's a God." Andy made a beeline toward a sideboard covered with urns of coffee and tea, platters of pastries.

Daphne, damn near sprinting to keep up, whispered, "Can't we stop at some off-the-road place instead?" All she needed was someone to stare at her a bit too long, think something about her looked familiar....

"It's free, baby. I never pass up a free meal."

They were at the sideboard. The scent of coffee and warm bread made her salivate. "Okay, but make it fast."

"Fast is my middle name."

"Really? I thought it was Humble."

He slid her a look, then poured coffee into two foam cups. "Cream?"

"Any nonfat milk?"

"Yeah, sure. And probably some goat cheese and porcelain mushrooms, too."

"Porcini."

"Whatever." He poured cream from a silver pitcher into her cup. Then he grabbed a few rolls, dropped them into his fleece pullover pocket.

"What are you doing?"

He picked up a few pats of butter and dropped them into his pocket, too. "Getting our breakfast."

"Can't you wrap those in a napkin or something?"

"Napkins. Good idea." He grabbed a few paper triangles with Inn at Maiden Falls scripted in gold, and shoved them into another pocket. "Okay, let's split." He took a step toward the main lobby doors.

Daphne grabbed his arm.

He turned to face her. "What?"

She wriggled her eyebrows toward the main doors. "State Representative Gerard and his wife," she whispered.

Andy glanced over his shoulder, recognizing the man in the three-piece suit, his arm around a stylishly dressed woman. They were laughing with another couple. He turned back to Daphne. "Friends of yours?"

"Gordo and I have socialized with them. Dinners, political functions. I can't chance their recognizing me." She stifled a groan. "Especially dressed like *this*."

He looked into her sunglasses, vaguely seeing the outline of those hazel eyes he'd come to know so well, and felt a sudden, irrational jolt of anger. "Embarrassed to be seen with me?"

Her shapely eyebrows pressed together. "Are you crazy?"

"Let's just say I don't like being the 'other man.'"

Her glossed pink lips fell open for a solid moment before she whispered, "You are *not* the 'other man.' Do you see a ring on my finger?" She held up her hand, manicured fingers splayed, before dropping it and muttering, "I can't believe we're having this conversation. We haven't even had sex."

Next to them, an elderly woman in a tweed suit stiffened, her hand frozen in midair over a basket of rolls.

"For the record," Andy said between his teeth, "I don't sleep with women who belong to other men."

Daphne fisted her hands on her hips. "Well," she whispered, *"for the record,* I don't belong—" She paused, stared at the elderly woman who was leaning so far toward them, she was darn near teetering to keep her balance.

Daphne looked back at Andy. "Can we please leave?" she asked tightly.

"We could," he said equally tightly, "except your fiancé's friends are blocking the entrance."

Daphne touched her tongue to her lip, staring at him. "You're jealous."

"Damn right."

One side of her mouth twitched in a smile. "Then stop playing hard to get and make me yours."

He snorted. "Lady, nobody can make *you* do anything and you know it."

Daphne edged closer, so close he could smell that wicked rose scent, see the slight flare of her nostrils.

"You can make me," she whispered, her breath hot on his cheek. "You can make me do *anything*."

The woman emitted an "oh my" and dropped her butter knife. It clattered on the table.

"Wonderful," Andy muttered, handing Daphne her coffee. "And you're the one who didn't want to make a scene." He put his hand on Daphne's back and steered her toward the historical parlor.

A few moments later, they stood alone in the parlor behind the red velvet rope. "I'm surprised someone didn't have to resuscitate that little old lady after your steamy comment."

"Did I embarrass you?" Daphne took a sip of her coffee.

"No."

"Would you like me to?"

Andy gave her a double take. "Did you put something in your drink when I wasn't looking?"

"Just playing with you."

Like a cat with its mouse. He eyed the front doors. "Doesn't that Gerard fellow have better things to do than chat up potential voters?" He looked around, his gaze stopping on a door at the back of the parlor. "Saw a housekeeper exit through here yesterday. Let's check it out."

Andy opened the door, barely able to breathe he was so damned worked up. If anyone had ever told him he'd get a raging hard-on in the lobby of a five-star hotel—a *honeymoon* hotel—with a woman dressed like L. L. Bean on acid, he would have said they'd lost their mind.

But that was before he'd met the hard-headed, hot-minded Daphne Remington, and lordy, lordy, he had a feeling his life was never going to be the same.

He looked over the velvet rope into the lobby. Besides the little old lady who was *still* staring at them, a roll clutched in her fist, no one else seemed to know they existed. He grabbed Daphne's free hand, tugged her inside, and shut the door.

They stood for a moment, listening to their breathing as their eyes adjusted to the gloom. Small pinpoints of light dotted the walls next to a staircase to their left. To their right was a darkened alcove.

Andy stepped into it, spied a silvery line of sunlight along the bottom of a door. Good. Their exit to outside.

He'd started to open it when he caught the scent of lilacs...sweet, enticing, igniting hot memories of last night, how Daphne's body had fit against his. Yielding, warm...

Make me yours.

He turned and stepped back into the stairwell.

A patch of sunlight streamed through a small window high in the wall, its rays highlighting Daphne's face. Everything was covered—her eyes behind those shades, her hair underneath that cap—making that curvaceous mouth more obvious. Something about her eyes being unreadable, but her mouth so exposed, challenged his passion.

"Let me take that," he said, easing the cup from her hand. He set their coffees on a stair, then turned back to her.

He moved close, so close he could almost touch her lips with his. "You keep toying with me," he whispered, his voice low, dark, as he fought to keep himself in check.

Her breath caught. "Yes," she whispered.

His gaze lowered to her mouth. That soft, sweet mouth that he was crazy to feel against his own again. He bit back the sharp taste of desire as his gaze lowered, inch by sensual inch, over her body. Down the soft, clinging flannel that outlined her breasts, taking his time to admire the subtlety of their shape underneath his shirt. Round. Full.

His gaze dropped farther and he eyed the play of muted light between her legs. The shadowed curve, a dark indentation. He inhaled deeply, imagining her scent.

He raised his gaze, studying the darkness behind her sunglasses. "I want you."

Upstairs, a door slammed.

Daphne looked up. "Somebody might—"

With a low growl, he stopped her words with a long, rough kiss. She tasted like coffee and sin, so hot and wet, and he took what he'd been craving for these long, long hours. Pressing himself against her, he murmured his secret desires against her panting lips before forcing them apart with his tongue and plunging inside, tasting her with slick, sensual strokes.

A low moan broke from deep in her throat and he ripped loose his mouth and plundered the soft hollow of her throat, licking and nibbling her silky skin as she whispered his name in breathless, pleading gasps.

She arched her back, pressing her mounds forward, and trailed her fingers down her front, pausing on her breast and idly circling the spot where her nipple lay beneath the shirt.

A hot wave swept through him and he grabbed the neck of the T-shirt with his teeth, ready to rip it loose.

Footsteps on the stairs above.

They paused, their bodies wracked with heaving breaths.

"We should go," Daphne said on a gasp.

Footsteps, louder.

He released his hold, tugged her trembling body to his. Pressing his lips to her ear, he whispered hotly, "You'll be mine."

Then he grabbed her hand, tugged her toward the alcove and pushed open the door. Cool mountain air assailed their heated bodies as they stumbled into the sunshine.

FROM THE historical parlor, Belle and a few of the girls stared out the bay window, watching Daphne and Andy as they darn near staggered down the street, hand in hand.

"Vas zat za gentleman who checked in alone?"

asked the Countess, fingering a brooch around her neck.

"Yes," said Belle, pleased with how things were going. And not going. The housekeepers in this place were too darn efficient, using the parlor stairs to skedaddle between floors. If Daphne and Andy had only had a minute or two more in that stairwell...

"Reckon Belle will be leavin' us soon," enthused Sunshine, sitting on the red velvet rope as though it were a swing. "Think of all those years we connived the golden rules, hopin' and praying somebody would buy this old place and make it a honeymoon hotel. Now here we are, fostering true love for all the fake love we made, getting ready to say goodbye to Belle, the first to earn ten notches."

Belle nodded. True, she'd done a dam—darn good job with these two strangers. From a sparkle of attraction to bursts of lust, although she didn't want them to consummate their passion *too* soon. Maybe it hadn't been such a bad thing for those housekeepers to be so darn tootin' efficient because before smoke turned to fire, Belle wanted Andy and Daphne to visit Charlie Remington's old place.

Where, Belle hoped, they'd discover more about Jo. She'd planted the image of her child in both their minds, sowed questions, too, about the child's history. Now she'd wait for their return, hear what they discovered.

Then they could rip loose, burn up all that pent-up passion.

She floated slowly out of the room and through the lobby, ignoring Flo, the ol' biddy, havin' one of her conniption fits about strumpets and their guns. Like Belle had the heart to do some target practice. If she did, she'd set her sights on Flo for a change.

Gliding up the stairs as she'd done a hundred, a thousand times, Belle thought how just as often she'd yearned for the day she'd be free. Never dreaming one day she'd bargain with hell itself to stay for an extra minute, an hour to learn the fate of her lost baby.

8

DAPHNE STARED out the passenger window as Andy steered the Jeep over the winding road of Guanella Pass, the main access between Maiden Falls and Last Chance, the name of Charles's mining claim, which the town had kept.

Last Chance. How many times had her family bragged about the history of the Remington dynasty, the long line of Charlie's descendents—a string of doctors, lawyers, businessmen—as though they were of royal blood, when, in fact, their careers were funded by a man who'd staked a claim with a to-hell-with-it-here-goes name because he was ready to throw in the towel and give up.

If someone had told him his last chance would build an empire, wonder what he would have thought?

Funny, how some thirty-some-odd hours ago, Daphne had felt as though this weekend were her last chance, too. As she'd hopped on that tour bus, she'd felt as though this excursion was her last chance for fun, freedom, her last chance to be herself.

Daphne looked at the scenery, the same views Charles himself must have witnessed over a hundred years ago. Green was sprouting on trees and hills, patches of snow crested distant peaks, and above it all a vast, endless blue sky. Daphne had always thought the spring skies in Colorado, especially up here in the mountains, were near perfection—a pristine blue, so clear and pure you almost ached looking at them. She closed her eyes and breathed deeply, taking in the pungent scent of earth, tangy pine, sweet hints of flowers. But best of all were the rushes of cool mountain air, bracing and invigorating.

Not cool enough, however, to quell that hot interlude in the stairwell back at the inn.

You'll be mine.

Hoo, boy. And the way Andy had said it—rough, demanding—it was a miracle she could even think straight with those words still sizzling in her brain.

She opened her eyes, daring to sneak a glance at Andy next to her.

Sunlight poured through the windshield, dusting him with gold. Unfair. The guy was sinful enough without fairy dust sprinkled on his manly self. Her gaze moved down his red fleece jacket, liking how his broad shoulders pressed against the fabric, down to his hands, brown and strong, that gripped the steering wheel as he confidently navigated the switchbacks.

She drew in a ragged breath, looked away. Suddenly the view of the Rockies and the boundless sky didn't hold as much appeal. Downright boring, in fact.

She looked back.

Hellloooo, handsome. She smiled, drinking him in. He was so preoccupied traversing these narrow, winding roads, she could just kick back and enjoy the view, the one next to her.

Up to now, everything had felt so hectic or weird or too hot to handle, she'd never really had a chance simply to observe the man. In a way, he looked like a leprechaun with that wild, red hair and mischievous air. Not your garden-variety leprechaun, but one with a devilishly sensual streak. The kind a woman would fall into bed with because she knew some wonderfully wicked things were in store.

And then there was that small, white scar on his chin. Wonder how he got that? From its color, it had to be something that happened years ago. She could imagine Andy as a kid, doing something insane like skydiving off a roof or crash-racing his bike.

But knowing his mother wasn't always available, it suddenly saddened Daphne to wonder who helped him when he was hurt or lonely. He'd probably learned to suck it up and be tough at a very young age. Learned to be resourceful, too. Most boys balked at household chores like taking out the trash, but she bet Andy did that and more. Maybe cooked meals, cleaned house, helped his mother when she couldn't help herself.

No wonder he was so watchful of Daphne. Or that's how she felt, anyway, that he quietly kept tabs, always making sure she was doing okay. She recalled the women at Mrs. Allen's regretting the burden they'd put on their kids. The guilt they carried for making them grow up faster than they should have.

Now Andy's love of books made sense. Not that it didn't before, it was just that Daphne had wondered how such a rough-and-tumble guy had learned to love dusty ol' classics. But now that she thought about it, this was the kind of kid who'd desperately needed an escape from his home life and he'd found it in books. Checked them out by the armful from the library, she'd bet, quickly graduating from children's books to the classics.

In her mind's eye, she could see Andy now, lying under the covers with a flashlight and falling into stories of pirates and intergalactic heroes and Don Quixote brandishing a lance at windmills, believing in the integrity of Dulcinea.

What had Andy said about Dulcinea? She was the personification of Don Quixote's dream?

Daphne had to look away again, this time because she didn't want Andy glancing over, seeing the emotion in her eyes. As a kid, he'd probably yearned to admire his mother despite the circumstances of her addiction. Daphne had often witnessed that at the halfway house. Yes, some kids were bitter, but others were hopeful. They didn't need to say it because their bright, shiny eyes said it all. They wanted desperately to believe everything would work out, that there'd be the happy ending promised in stories.

Suddenly the image of fairy dust didn't seem so far-fetched. Andy deserved that happy ending, and Daphne hoped fervently she'd be the one he'd share it with.

TEN MINUTES LATER, they pulled up in front of a picturesque Victorian home, meticulously restored with its richly detailed mansard roof, dormer windows and a charming turret Daphne recalled Charles had added especially for his bride. Around the house was a pristine white picket fence, upon which hung a sign that read "The Charles Remington House" and underneath "National Register of Historic Places."

"Nice digs," Andy said. He opened his door, jumped down, and headed around to Daphne's side.

He opened her door. She sat there, windblown curls escaping underneath her baseball cap, giving him the strangest look.

"You okay?"

She quirked a smile. "Yes, just thinking about things."

"Like?"

"Oh, Don Quixote...Dulcinea..."

His chivalrous impulses kicking into gear, Andy swept her into his arms and lowered her to the ground. "And...?"

Hints of her rose perfume tangled with scents of lavender and pine. He kept his hands around her middle, liking the indentation of her waist, the softness of her underneath the clothes. "Thought you hated the classics."

"Well, yes, but you helped me understand some of the deeper meaning in the story."

Her mouth wreathed into the sweetest smile and for a moment, he chided himself for his earlier L. L. Bean thought. Daphne looked pretty darn cute in his Rockies cap and his favorite flannel shirt.

"So," he said, reluctantly releasing his hold, "what about Quixote and Dulcinea?"

"He, uh, had a dream." Daphne slid her arm through his and they began walking toward the Remington House.

"The impossible dream."

"Maybe not that impossible," she murmured.

When they reached the gate, Andy unlatched it, gestured for Daphne to enter first. As a breeze gusted past, flipping the tail of her flannel shirt, he copped a look at her tush. For a class act, she could sure jiggle booty.

His gaze dropped down a pair of long lean legs, past the point where cloth gave way to bare, shapely calves, to the craziest pair of neon-green heels he'd ever seen in his life.

He closed the gate behind them, giving his head a shake. Women and fashion. Frank had once forced Andy to slap together a quick and dirty story on a winter fashion show after another writer had quit in a huff. Andy had thrown together a piece on faux fur and what just might be faux, too, on Pamela Anderson Lee, a big PETA supporter. After Frank had popped a few Xanax and tossed the piece into his trash can, he'd eighty-sixed Andy from further fashion assignments.

Which was cool with Andy. He'd love to be eighty-sixed from writing more damn fluff pieces, too, like this honeymoon hotel thing. Which he'd pretty much avoided writing up until now. At least he'd grabbed some brochures off the inn's registration desk, so technically he'd done *some* research.

Being here in Last Chance and visiting the old Remington home was *much* more Andy's style. He could spend the rest of his life studying Colorado history and never get bored. Plus here he was visiting a historical site with one of the original owner's descendants. Hell, if his granddad, who'd inspired Andy's love of western history, knew his grandson was getting "mighty comfortable"—as Gramps would say— with a Remington, well, Andy could almost hear the old man chuckling all the way from heaven.

"Listen," Daphne said when they reached the front door. "I'm not saying I'm a Remington."

"Because of how you're dressed and because you're with me?"

"You, who is *not* the other man." She gave his hand a squeeze.

"Baby, keep this up and I'll start believing you."

She slipped her sunglasses off, those hazel eyes flashing him a pleased look. "Well, *now* you're talkin', Mr. Sweet Talkin' Guy."

He walked inside, a six-foot-two guy suddenly ten feet tall.

Minutes later, they were ambling through the rooms, listening to a Grand Dame—or as she'd introduced herself, a member of the National Society of the Colonial Dames of America, chatter about the history of the home. Words fascinated Andy, and he pondered the significance of a group of women referring to themselves as "grand dames."

Which he decided had something to do with their perfume, because this one had splashed on so much, she smelled like eau de grand fleur.

"And this room," she said with a sweep of a pudgy hand riddled with rings, "is part of the west wing addition of 1893, the year Charles Remington struck gold. It was designed for the many guests who traveled by the Colorado Central Railroad to do business with the young, suddenly rich, magnate."

"He and his young bride must have been inundated with money and people," said Daphne.

The Grand Dame nodded. Through her bifocals, an oversize tear glistened. Andy couldn't help but wonder if Grand Dames felt a bit too overly responsible for the world.

"They hired a young housekeeper to help out," she said, solemnly. "From what we glean from the records of the time, she and her husband had run a store and given young Charles and his bride supplies during their lean years. The husband had died of yellow fever in '91, so after Charles struck it rich, he and Sarah opened up their home, offering the widow a job as their housekeeper."

Daphne flashed a knowing look at Andy.

"On the ceiling," the Grand Dame continued, gesturing upward with a flourish, "you see the original chandelier with its green gaslight shades." She looked back down at them. "Electricity was installed the following year, although by then Charles was making plans to move his family to Denver."

Andy pulled a notepad out of his pocket and jotted down a few things.

"And on the far wall," the Grand Dame said, heading in that direction, "are a series of photographs of Charles and his family and associates prior to and after he struck gold. In this one, dated 1894, the last year they lived in Last Chance, you'll see a family Christmas gathering in this very room." She motioned to the floor. "By then, he'd installed the exquisite maple and walnut flooring we're standing on today—" she gestured to the table "—and over there are pieces of his elegant Haviland china from Limoges."

She stepped back, inviting Andy and Daphne to take a closer look at the photograph. "See those large mirrors on the wall? They're diamond-dust mirrors, the backing isn't silver, but crushed diamonds which gives them an exquisitely clear reflection, almost as though you can step inside. Charles, who had a romantic streak, named the largest mirror 'Lady of the Lake,' a reference, of course, to the water deity in the Arthurian legend."

She straightened, then smiled sadly. "Unfortunately, that mirror was lost over the years. Some say it

was stolen—which makes sense as the diamond c
made those mirrors extremely valuable. Others s
Charles gave it as a gift to his housekeeper on her
wedding day."

"Wedding day?" exclaimed Daphne.

"She remarried?" said Andy.

The Grand Dame, who'd maintained a rather stern
expression up to now, suddenly looked surprised.
"Why, yes."

"When?" asked Daphne.

"I believe soon after the Remingtons moved to Denver."

"1894," confirmed Andy, jotting it down.

"Who did she marry?" asked Daphne.

The dame drew in her lips thoughtfully. "I don't
rightly know. No one's ever asked before. But..." She
looked thoughtful for a moment. "I recall once hearing she married a wagoner—our modern-day equivalent of a truck driver, except he drove some kind of
freight wagon—and they moved to...St. Louis?
Omaha?" She shrugged. "Sorry, I don't exactly recall."

From another room came a tinkling sound, the bell
that rang whenever the front door opened.

The Grand Dame smiled apologetically. "I need to
greet new visitors."

"If you don't mind," Daphne said, "we'd like to
look at the rest of the photographs, finish the tour on
our own."

"Certainly. There are write-ups on the wall next to

photo, providing some history, names. In the
rooms, we ask that you don't enter the roped-off
areas and please don't touch the wall covering—it's
the original Lincrusta Walton with refinished silver
and gold relief. Otherwise, guests are welcome to
walk around. If you have any other questions, I'll be
happy to answer them at the end of your tour." And,
in a swirl of movement, the Grand Dame swept out of
the room.

"That's some dame," Andy murmured after they
were alone.

Daphne grinned. "Well, on their behalf, I should
mention they're all volunteers."

"Make me feel guilty." He glanced around. "Guess
it's out of the question to ask if I can smoke?"

"In a historical building, made of wood, over a hundred years old?"

"I take that to be a no."

She gave in to a smile. "You're a rascal."

"I'm coming up in the world. I used to be impudent."

"Still are."

"Only if you want me to be."

Daphne curled her toes, as though that would
ground her, because he was giving her *that* look, the
one he'd given her in the stairwell, and now wasn't
the time to liquidate into a hormonal pool of hot, do-
me need.

Her heart thudding dully, Daphne glanced back at
the photograph. Even if her libido was ready to bolt,

the rest of her body wanted to stay here just a little while longer, try to learn something more about the housekeeper and her child. "Wonder what the house-keeper's name was?"

"Let's read the write-up," Andy said, moving closer. Daphne caught his scent, masculine, a hint of soap from his morning shower. "Here we go...left to right, there's Charles and his wife Sarah, some gentle-man named James Dexter—"

"Another struck-it-rich fellow from Leadville."

"And Elizabeth Sutherland with her baby, Jo."

They both were quiet for a moment, taking in that last piece of information.

"Well," Andy said straightening. "We have a last name."

"Elizabeth's *first* married name. We don't know the wagoner's."

"We can always research her name on the Internet."

"And the baby's. Maybe Jo kept her biological fa-ther's name."

"Let's wrap up the tour, head back," suggested Andy. "We have some work ahead of us."

Daphne put her hand on his sleeve. "I know I'm cu-rious about this child, but you have other things to do. Like write your honeymoon hotel article."

"As I said, I can do that in my sleep. Doing histori-cal research is the kind of stuff I love." He snapped his fingers. "Got it! I'll kick off the interview with that photograph, the search for the child. Segue into the search for the real Daphne Remington, the rich girl with the heart of gold. I'll ask questions about your work with the halfway house, your photographs. You know, those are particularly fascinating, Daphne. Do you realize how your photos have helped the women bridge relationships not only with their families, but with the community?"

Daphne blinked in surprise. "Don't you think you're, uh, giving my photos more weight than they deserve?"

Andy turned her toward him, his hands on her shoulders. "Let me say it another way. Your talent helped other women rebuild their self-esteem. Time someone took that same interest in you."

"Through an interview?" she asked incredulously.

"Good place to start." He slipped his notepad into his jacket pocket. "Next, a showing of your photographs. Hell, why not shoot for a book someday, too?"

She scoffed, fighting a surge of anger she didn't understand. She wanted to snap something about pie-in-the-sky dreams or certain men with delusional thinking, but then she recalled how he'd looked bathed in sunshine, as though covered in the sheen of fairy dust, and suddenly her mind and body stilled.

This was a man who believed in dreams, and the anger she felt wasn't at him.

It was at herself. For not believing in herself.

Daphne felt momentarily stunned at the realization. She wanted to say something, but the breath caught in her lungs. And if she could have pulled it together enough to speak what was on her heart, she'd say,

"Thank you for looking beneath what everyone else sees."

Instead, she raised her hand and touched a fingertip to the jagged white scar on his chin and thought how sweet it would be to be part of this man's life for a long time, to take care of him, just as she instinctively knew he'd take care of her, in the ways that truly mattered. Their physical health, their emotional well-being, their dreams...

As though he could read her thoughts, he moved closer and slipped his arms around her. She sank against him, the silence that fell over them complete, fulfilling, broken only by the distant sound of wind soughing through trees, the sound eerily similar to the falls slowly thawing.

When she finally found her voice, she whispered, "Andy Branigan, you're a prince of a guy."

He chuckled, the sound low and rumbling in his chest. "A prince and his princess," he murmured.

He pulled her back at arms' distance, searched her face, and she marveled at the depth in his blue eyes, as endless as the Colorado skies. And she knew they'd just shifted into a new part of their relationship, one that held the sweet promise of many tomorrows.

"Let's finish the tour and this discussion later," Andy finally said.

They exited the room, walked down the hallway and turned into a doorway.

And halted in their tracks.

Across the room, curtains fluttered on a breeze.

Through the open window could be seen the Rockies, those panoramic Colorado skies, and nearer, trees bursting with white flowers.

Apple trees.

"Andy," Daphne whispered.

"I know."

They were staring at the kitchen where they'd made love in the dream.

"WHY IN *that* house? *That* kitchen?" asked Daphne, tossing her sunglasses onto the marble-topped table.

"Because..." The moment they'd returned to their room, Andy had made a beeline to his backpack, withdrawn a flask and taken a healthy swig. Finished, he wiped his mouth and exhaled deeply. "Because," he repeated, "for some reason, we were supposed to be there." He handed the flask to Daphne.

She nodded, as though that made sense—*not*—and accepted the flask. "Vodka, right?"

"Last I checked."

She took a sip, coughed, took another. She needed to brace herself. That whole kitchen extravaganza had been just a titch too much. They'd been shocked, to put it mildly, after their mutual realization that the kitchen at Charlie's home was the same as the one in their dream. It'd been so many years since she'd visited her ancestor's home, years and years with *several* restoration projects in the interim, there's no way she could've resurrected the image of that kitchen from a memory.

After leaving the house, she and Andy had managed a few awkward sentences, but with the wind rushing through the Jeep's windows, it'd been too difficult to try and conduct a conversation.

"So," she continued, plopping down on the love seat, "let's assume for some far-fetched, high woo-woo reason, we were *supposed* to be there. Dream-wise and real-wise. Oh hell, I need another drink." She helped herself.

Andy stared out the bay window. "We had a child."

Ah, yes. The child. In her dream—well, his, too—Andy had asked about the child's whereabouts, and she'd answered that he—she?—was at a neighbor's and they'd taken advantage of those stolen moments to make love, right there in the kitchen.

A child...

She played with the bare spot on her ring finger. Funny, she and Gordo hadn't really talked about children all that much. Oh, they'd discussed it in vague terms, using words like *someday* but it seemed so many other things took precedence—his law practice, his political career. And being the new-and-improved Daphne, the one who never rocked the boat anymore, she'd gone along with the agenda.

Except, she suddenly had a different agenda. Her own. One where her needs mattered, too. When she got back to Denver, first on her list was to talk things over with Gordo, explain she'd never really be the right one for him, or him for her, here's the ring, we can always be friends...

It felt sad, but also right. In the long run, they'd both be much happier.

She took another sip, then jiggled the flask at Andy. "Did we call our child by name?"

"No." Andy crossed the room, took the proffered flask.

"What if it was...Jo?"

Andy stopped, feeling as though he'd been hit by lightning. He took a sip. A long one.

"You know," he finally said, "I've been thinking that Jo was born about the same time Belle 'disappeared' on her trek from Tombstone to Maiden Falls..." He let his voice trail off, because his mind was chewing on other things.

Like how he'd always thought he'd never have his own kids.

Because, if he was totally honest with himself, he had this gut-deep fear he'd somehow alienate the child or not be around enough or do something stupid that would mess up the kid's life forevermore. Andy had actually talked to a shrink once about this, someone he was interviewing for a story, and she'd said her perception was that Andy was worrying about nothing; in fact, his worrying showed he cared and had the makings to be a good father.

He'd changed the subject after that.

Hell, if a date had even *hinted* at family and kids, he'd not only change the subject but find a way to put an end to things, fast.

And then Daphne had wandered into his life and

suddenly everything felt different. Fresh, exciting, *alive*. And the more he got to know her, the more he discovered that being with her felt a hell of a lot better than being alone.

He'd even caught himself wondering what it'd be like to experience more with this woman. Not just making love—which he wanted so badly his body was on permanent ache—but wondering what it'd be like to wake up every morning with this woman, to share life's joys...

...to have a child.

He looked down at Daphne, sprawled comfortably on the love seat, those crazy lime-green shoes, the baseball cap tilted sideways.

"Take off your hat," he said gently.

She looked up at him, her eyes glistening, and slowly removed the cap. Wild curls fell about her face, her cheeks tinged pink.

"I like your freckles," he murmured, stepping closer.

She scrunched shut her eyes. "I hate them."

"Shame." He moved closer. "Because every single part of you should be adored."

Getting down on one knee, he framed her face with his hands and she slowly opened her eyes. His thumbs brushed her cheekbones, then moved up to trace the few specks across the bridge of her nose, before moving to the corners of her lips.

"I want to..."

"Me, too."

He closed his eyes, debating how to phrase his next question delicately. "Do you—" he looked at her again "—have any protection?"

She shrugged apologetically. "No. Didn't think I'd be needing it."

"No problem. I have something in my car." Glove compartment was a damn inconvenient place to keep condoms, but he hadn't thought he'd be needing them, either.

He got off his knee, stood. "Be right back."

Alone, Daphne stared at the closed door, knowing she probably had the goofiest smile on her face, but damn, that's exactly how she felt. Goofy, happy and so horny, that poor man wouldn't know what hit him when he got back.

I need to formally end it with Gordo, tell him it's over, before...

She crossed to the phone on the nightstand, punched in Gordo's cell phone number.

"Gordon here."

She rolled her eyes, hating how he'd taken to answering the phone in that all-business, Mr. Politician voice.

"Hi, it's Daphne—"

"Where are you?"

"Uh, out of town."

"The Inn at Maiden Falls?"

Oops. The name of the hotel must be flashing on his caller ID. All the more reason to cut to the chase.

"Gordo, you and I both know things between us

have been...strained. I'm not happy and neither are you—"

"I'm happy."

About the unhappiest-sounding words from a happy man she'd ever heard. At that precise moment, she knew her status as a Remington was worth far more than her true self, which only strengthened her resolve.

"You'll do much better without me, Gordo, and I know there's a woman who'll love being—" stifled, suffocated "—supportive of your political career. I'm giving you back your ring when I return to Denver."

Pause. "Daphne, you've been under a lot of stress. Let's give this a chance, talk it over—"

"It's for the best, Gordo, for both of us." She hung up the phone, fighting a stab of guilt. Maybe she hadn't handled that with the greatest panache, but at least she'd been honest.

Brring. Brring.

Damn. He's calling back.

Brring. Brring.

She eased in a calming breath. Well, she *had* been somewhat abrupt. Wouldn't hurt to clarify her position, if nothing else.

"Hello?"

"Hello, doll."

Doll? Had to be Andy. Maybe calling from the lobby to see if she'd like some chilled champagne to go with their hot lovin'?

"Hello, handsome." She smiled to herself, liking this love play.

A throaty laugh, deeper than Andy's. "Is our boy around?"

"Our boy?" Her stomach flip-flopped.

"Right. Andy. Tell him Frank, his editor, is calling."

Shock waves rolled through her. Sure, Andy had mentioned Frank several times, but Andy had also sworn Frank didn't know about her. Didn't know she was here, in this room. But to listen to Frank say "Hello, doll" without even missing a beat, he obviously knew more than Andy had let on.

"He'll get the message." She hung up the phone, the click as sharp as the knife of betrayal she felt in her heart.

9

"DOLL?" Daphne asked, her arms crossed under her breasts.

Andy, who'd just stepped back into the bedroom, stared at her. "Yes, hon?"

"Frank,' she said coolly, *too* coolly, "called me 'doll.'"

"Frank?" The edge of the condom box was digging a hole into Andy's thigh, but considering Daphne's thoroughly pissed-off look, pulling out a box of condoms wasn't exactly the smoothest move a man could make at a moment like this.

"Yes, *Frank*," Daphne confirmed, narrowing her eyes. "You told him about me."

"What?"

"You gave me your *word*, told me *no* one would know I was staying here, then you blabbed it to an *editor*—" She raised a sardonic eyebrow as though her chilling tone didn't adequately convey the sense of imminent doom. "No, not just an editor, but a-a—"

"Features editor." Andy couldn't believe he was having this bizarre argument over the exact wording of his boss's job title, not to mention *with* a frickin' painful box of condoms in his pocket.

"Right, *features* editor at the *Denver Post*—"

"Daphne, he knew I was writing an interview with you, well, not exactly with *you*, but with *someone*, and that I was doing it on my own time. I don't get the problem here. You agreed to the interview."

"I agreed as long as you *waited* until *after* this weekend before telling the *Post*. That Frank fellow didn't miss a beat when I answered the phone. Not even an *instant* of surprise when he heard my voice." Daphne gave a snort of derision. "You know, you could have caused *less* damage riding up and down the streets of Denver blasting the news through a megaphone about ol' wild-at-heart Renegade Remington on the loose again, but noo. *You* call the *features editor* at the *Post!* Because, hey, it's hot-off-the-press news of my rowdy, raucous, reprehensible—"

"Aren't you getting a bit carried away?"

"—*renegade* self—and don't tell me I'm getting carried away. You—you *Post* people love those *R* words when it comes to us Remingtons. A slew of *R* words is probably smeared all over the front page even as we speak—"

"It would be on the features page, if anywhere," he muttered, knowing as soon as he uttered the words he'd just stuck one big fat foot into his even bigger, fatter mouth.

"Front, features, what's the diff?" she said, her voice rising to a pitch that probably had canines in the next county pricking their ears. "Renegade Remington rides again!"

She certainly had a way with words when she was worked up. If he wasn't so damn crazy about her, and damn protective, too, despite her holier-than-thou act she was pulling off right now, he'd steal that headline himself.

But first things first. He wanted to help her calm down so they could talk reasonably, so she'd understand no damage was done.

"Daphne, sweetheart, you're overreacting—"

She sputtered something incoherent, her arms flailing, before belting out, "Easy for *you* to say! You, who can live a life without being under the scrutiny of everybody's damn microscope—"

"Daphne!" He took a step toward her and winced. This box of condoms was going to cause permanent damage if he didn't get it out soon.

Fortunately, she mistook his moment of pained silence as a moment of acquiescence because suddenly she looked calmer. Not less sanctimonious, but definitely calmer.

"I don't begrudge my family's money," she said nobly, "because it's given me a lot, but it's also taken away any pretense of *ever* living a normal life."

Her chin started to quiver, her eyes shining with emotion. He walked toward her, arms open, thinking, praying, hoping, this moment of insanity was finally over.

"No." She backed away. "I need a moment to myself, *alone*. If you get any closer, I won't be able to think... I'll just succumb to my primal, animalistic needs, which is the *last* thing I should be doing."

Last? Now his chin was quivering, his eyes welling with emotion. When the two of them got their act together—and he meant *together*—he was going to have a serious talk with her about life's priorities.

"I'm going to take a bath," she said quietly. "A long, hot one."

He could have done without the "long, hot" part. "And then we'll talk," he said. "Because I promise you, Frank doesn't know it's you—"

But, as Tony Soprano might have said, bada-bing she was gone. Disappeared into the bathroom, door shut.

Click.

And locked.

Andy stood there, blew out a puff of air, tugged the box of condoms out of his too-tight pants pocket and tossed them onto the nightstand. So all this was over Frank calling her doll? Hell, Frank called *everyone* doll. He'd even called Andy doll once, but it'd been late, in a dark corner in a bar, and Frank had been on his fourth martini.

"I'm gonna kill Frank," Andy muttered, the sounds of rushing water coming from behind the bathroom door as Daphne filled the tub.

He fought images of her slipping off her clothes—hell, she probably wore those black lacy-stretchy-see-through bras with matching stretchy undies—getting

naked, testing the water temperature with her sucka-
ble red-tipped toes...

Swish swish swish.

He flashed on smug, doll-faced Frank again. *I'll
strangle him with my bare hands.*

A few minutes later, Andy hung up the receiver,
having given Frank a no-nonsense, tight-lipped up-
date on the honeymoon hotel story. He skipped the
part about wanting to strangle him because, well,
there was the little issue of this deadline and Frank's
required signature on his payroll check.

Instead, Andy promised he'd have part one of the
honeymoon hotel story uploaded by tonight, so best to
get right on it. He could get most of what he needed
from the brochure and a few phone calls, but it
wouldn't hurt to walk around a bit and ask questions
of the staff.

Andy started to leave, paused, then marched to the
closed bathroom door and raised his hand to knock.

And paused.

Good God Almighty, scents from the Casbah were
emanating from within. Heady, sweet. Like almonds
and honey. He could just imagine that scent slathered
over naked, slippery skin.

May you rot in hell, Frank.

Maybe she was calmer. He should try to explain
again. "Daphne?"

A light splashing sound. "What?"

"Frank, uh, doesn't know who you are."

Silence.

"He calls everybody doll."

More silence.

"In bad lighting, he'd call Janet Reno doll."

"Like *that's* supposed to make me feel better?"

At least she's talking to me. "So, uh, while you're soaking—" he squeezed shut his eyes, fighting images of naked pink flesh covered with shiny bubbles that could *pop pop pop*, giving way to an even better view of naked pink flesh "—I'm going to leave the room and wrap up my research," he rasped. "Be back in a few to type up my notes."

Splash splash.

With a weighty sigh, he left. Trudging down the hall, he muttered, "What the hell am I doing here? I should just wrap up my research and drive straight back to Denver."

Because he had zero desire to spend his last night in a big-bedded, mirrored-wall hotel room made for hot love when all he was gonna get was the cold shoulder.

"HELL'S BELLS," muttered Belle, floating after him. She looked upward. Good. Miss Arlotta hadn't caught that slip of the tongue. But dang it all anyway, now Andy was ready to leave and Daphne was locked inside the bathroom.

These two were the orneriest pair Belle had *ever* met, and considering the hundred-plus years she'd been haunting these haunts, so to speak, that was saying a lot.

Andy stomped down the staircase and flagged

down the manager. She smiled professionally as Andy approached and flipped open his notepad, ready to start interviewing.

Belle flitted toward the lobby where some of the girls lounged about. She'd keep an eye on Andy from here, reel him back in should he get that cockamamie idea to return to Denver again.

"What's happenin', Miss Belle?" asked Mimi, eternally winsome in her lace-trimmed French chemise.

"Bidin' my time," Belle muttered, not wanting to let on things weren't going so well for her couple.

"Looks like your gent is all alone, chattin' it up with the manager," said Flo with a sniff.

"He's a reporter," Belle said calmly. "Doin' his research while his lady takes a long, hot bath." She gave the girls a knowing look, one that said sweet lovin' was next on the menu.

Rosebud suddenly looked over the edge of her book. "Maybe you should dip into your bag of tricks, Belle."

It took Belle aback for a moment, because Rosebud always preferred to keep her nose stuck in a book rather than get caught up in the girls' conversations, but when she spoke, there was always a good reason.

Which Belle got, loud and clear. It was time for her to quit merely "setting the scene" and play some of her magic with this couple. "You're right," she said with a nod, floating upward off a couch. "Time to use some of my love tricks."

She watched Andy, who was entering an elevator

with the manager. She was probably giving him a short tour, enough time for Belle to regroup, figure out her next move.

Belle floated up, up through several floors until she reached the roof. There, she glided over to the railing and looked down on the town of Maiden Falls and pondered her dilemma. The golden rules, as Miss Arlotta had reminded them many a time, were never meant to be easy. As she'd often said, "If ya reap what ya sow, you girls sowed plenty of marital discord in your day...which means you don't deserve things to be easy gettin' to the great beyond."

Belle took a puff of her cigarillo, watched its stream of smoke blend into the heavens above, and hoped that's where her little Jo ended up, the thought squeezing Belle's heart somethin' fierce.

If I had it all to do over again, I'd never have given you up. I'd have gone back to Tombstone and faced the music, because nothing matters but love. And just so's you know, honey, I gave your daddy the most love I'd ever been able to give any man....

The green leaves on the aspens shimmered with an invisible breeze as a hawk circled overhead. The back of Belle's neck tingled with an unseen presence.

At first she saw nothing, then the form of Drake appeared. A full materialization, as dapper and handsome as he'd been in 1889. The dark, drooping mustache that set off his obsidian eyes. And that smile...oh dear Lord, no man could match that smile.

Even now, all these lifetimes later, his mere presence touched her in a way that transcended the physical and reached down, soul-deep.

"Until you believe in true love, Bonnie," he said, his voice deep and rich, "I can't return to you, not fully. You must *truly* believe."

Truly believe? She wanted to cry out that that was exactly what she'd been doing here at the inn, inspiring couples to become even greater believers in the power of love.

But before she could respond, the edges of his hair faded, blending into the air until all that was left were his piercing eyes searching hers...

"No!" she choked, rushing forward. She threw forward her hands, cupping the contours of his face as though she could hold on to him forever...

And then she stood, her hands filled with air, the quiet rushing of the distant falls like a reminder that everything passes and is gone, gone so quickly.

"ANDY?" Daphne called from behind the closed bathroom door.

From where he sat on the bed, leaning against pillows as a backrest, he stopped typing. "What?"

"Uh, can you help me?"

He hit Save, stared at the bathroom door. "What?"

"You don't have to sound mad."

He rolled his eyes. How did she expect him to sound after he dashed outside for condoms, dashed back inside only to be told sex was off limits because someone had the audacity to call her doll? So he'd spent the last twenty minutes taking one hell of a bo-o-oring tour of the inn with the stodgy manager— exactly how a horny man wanted to spend his afternoon.

And now, Miss I'm-Naked-in-the-Tub-but-Tough-Luck-for-You wanted help? "Call 911," he grumped.

Splashing sounds. "Very funny."

He kept typing.

"Andy?"

He stopped. "Now what?"

"I, uh, *really* need help."

She did sound a little scared, but he was still a lot pissed. "What's the problem?"

"My, uh, toe is stuck in the faucet."

He paused, scratched his eyebrow. "Like I said, I'll call 911."

"No!"

She did sound rather pathetic and frantic, which made him feel a little bad for his snotty reply.

Just a little.

"What were you doing? Checking your toe size?"

More splashes. "If I told you, you wouldn't believe me."

No, I probably wouldn't. "So..." He shoved the laptop and his fleece pullover aside, rolled off the bed and stood, as though blood rushing to his feet might help him think better. "Want me to call room service? They probably have that kind of wine opener that doesn't screw into the cork, but slides down its sides."

Screw. That wine opener was a hell of a lot luckier than ol' Andy.

"No!"

He walked to the door, leaned his head against it. "Daphne, I realize you're having some kind of... predicament...but I don't carry toe-removal tools in my backpack, and besides *you* locked the frickin' bathroom door—"

His hand, which had been resting on the knob, suddenly slipped. The door clicked open.

Hell, he could have sworn he'd heard it lock earlier.

So, what kind of woman didn't *really* lock a door? Maybe, oh, a mule-headed one who's too proud to say "I'm sorry" and admit her desire for her, uh, roommate?

Andy had been teased by the best, and he could take just about anything dished out to him. But this little game of come-and-get-me, no-you-can't-have-me was enough to try a saint.

Fortunately, sainthood wasn't his thing. He started to open the door.

She shrieked. "Let me grab a faceclo—"

He stepped inside into some kind of hazy Shangri-la. The mist dampened his short-sleeved T-shirt, scented the room with a stimulating mixture of almonds and honey. Through the clearing haze, he saw her. A vision immersed in an old-fashioned porcelain tub brimming with sparkling bubbles, one slender leg poised midair...

...its *toe* wedged into the *faucet!*

He glanced back at her face, meaning to ask something, well, intelligent, like why did you stick your toe into the faucet? when his attention got snagged on that strip of terrycloth she'd managed to toss over her breasts.

Or, more exactly over *half* her breasts, leaving a plump, pert one gorgeously exposed. Pink and full and tipped with a dark, pebbled nipple.

And for a wickedly delicious moment, titillating images of what he'd like to do to that breast paraded through his mind like some kind of erotic slide show. Images of him massaging, kneading and leaning over to take one big mouthful of...

"My toe!" she shrieked, her face scrunched in a look of horror. "*Look* at it! It's wedged up there and what the hell am I doing to do?"

Right, the toe.

He looked back up to her face, summoning every ounce of willpower and common sense—which in an overly aroused male brain meant he had *zero*—to figure out what to do. Finally, a thought rose to the surface of his libido-frenzied mind, the way answers pop to the surface in an eight ball.

"Can I suck your breast?"

"What?" she shrieked, bolting half-upright, which she could have done all the way if her wedged toe wasn't seriously cramping her style.

"I mean—" Damn, damn, damn. "I mean, maybe if I sucked your *toe*. Or lathered it up. Or smeared cream all over it. Oh, for God's sake, let's just cut the whole thing off and call it a day."

If she'd looked horrified before, she looked downright hysterical now. "Wha—?"

"I'm kidding, I'm kidding." He swiped at his forehead, wishing he had a drink. Maybe this was a good time to raid the minibar, get reinforcements. No, what if he had one too many airplane bottles and tried to pry her toe loose with the wrong gadget on that Swiss knife he carried in his backpack...?

No, no, no. Minibar could wait. He was going to have to remain stone-cold sober for this operation.

"So, what happened?" he said in his best Dr. Toe voice.

She blew a bubble off her nose. "I was lying here, soaking, minding my own business, when suddenly, as though it had a will of its own, my leg lifted—" she raised her arms in a theatrical, lifting motion in case he might not know what "lifted" meant "—and the toe aimed *right* for the faucet and *stuck* itself in there."

He nodded, slowly, as though that made perfect sense. After his "Can I suck your breast?" comment, he would have played it super cool if she'd said a dozen little green men had landed in the bathroom and played tic-tac-toe with her toe.

"And, uh, when did you unlock the door so your toe could be rescued?"

Her mouth dropped open, then snapped shut. "It was locked all the time!"

"Uh-huh." The things a woman would do to get a

man into the bathroom. "Just curious," he said, eyeing her toe, "do you always stick appendages into little openings?"

"What?"

"You stuck your pinkie finger in that airplane bottle last night."

She gave him a dirty look. "You think I get my jollies going around sticking parts of my body in objects for the hell of it?"

A warning buzz in his brain told him not to say what he was thinking. In fact, not even to *think* what he was thinking. Instead, he knelt next to the tub and checked out the errant toe. It was stuck in there pretty solidly all right. He'd taken a lot of things out of a lot of places, but removing a toe was a first.

He looked around, doing his best not to stare at anything that might be peeking through the bubbles. "Where's the soap?"

She handed him a heart-shaped pink bar that looked more like a piece of candy.

"I'll, uh lather up your toe," he said, accepting it. "See if that works." He rubbed the soap around the toe, trying to slide bubbles between the stuck toe and the faucet opening as best he could.

"Try giving it a tug."

She did. Nothing.

He looked around the bathroom. "Any oils, creams in here?"

"I have some face cream in the cabinet. White jar, silver lid."

He found the jar, opened it and caught a whiff of gardenia that brought back searing memories of one particularly hot night in New Orleans with a very sexy lady ready to throw caution—and her clothes—to the wind on a carriage ride through the French Quarter.

These hot images burning through his brain had to stop. It was difficult enough to be crouched next to Daphne's lusciously naked body, smearing her toe with a creamy, gooey mixture without losing his frickin' mind.

"Okay," he croaked. "Try pulling again."

Nothing.

He looked at her, blinked. "I think we're going to have to call in reinforcements."

Her face caved in with a total look of humiliation. "I can't stand the thought of a bunch of people in here with me naked, everyone trying to extract my toe—"

She looked like about the saddest, wettest person he'd ever seen.

And sexiest.

He skimmed the surface of that bubbly water, catching wavering glimpses of pink skin and dark crevices. And at some point that soggy, body-molding facecloth had slid off her breast because now *both* were exposed.

"Maybe if you used a little more force," she said, her voice deeper, huskier than he remembered. "You know, braced yourself against the tub with one hand, you could use your other hand to help me tug the toe loose."

His senses engorged with scents of gardenia and almonds, he reached one hand under the water for support, biting back a groan when his fingers slid along wet flesh. Wet, firm flesh. Had to be her thigh. God, she had to be one of those women who wore those skintight pink thong contraptions while they pumped away on a treadmill, beads of sweat rolling down their skin, lodging in places best left to the imagination...

He tried to slide his fingers off her treadmill-toned thigh, fumbling for a place on the slick bottom of the tub where he could flatten his palm for support when her hand caught his underwater.

He looked at her as she held on to his hand and slipped her body down a little more into the water. Then, dear God, she bent her knees, those creamy bubble-dotted legs breaking the surface of the water enough that he caught a vision of a triangle of downy hairs wavering languidly, invitingly...

She was hostage, vulnerable, suspended by her toe for God's sake, and he felt guilty for all of, oh, a millisecond.

"You're beautiful," he breathed, still holding her hand underwater while his other stroked the crest of her knee, then inched all the way down her inner thigh until his fingers brushed that too-soft, silky triangle of hair.

She spread her knees wider, inviting him to go deeper. And, when he started to look back to the faucet—some far region of his mind saying there was a toe in crisis, right?—she undulated her hips, reminding him where his attention should be...

He struggled for breath as his sudsy hands slipped and slid down again, caressing her sleek thighs, buttocks. Busy, soapy fingers slithered between her cheeks, touched the perimeter of her triangle, brushed her downy mound. And when his hands slid upward to her stomach, those muscles flinched and she pressed her pelvis forward, pleading softly, "A little lower...please...please..."

He hesitated, glancing back for a split second at her toe.

Which was loose.

The red-tipped big toe was free, the sole of her foot braced along with its red-tipped brothers and sisters against the tiled wall next to the faucet.

The lady wasn't captive—had she ever truly been?—although she sure as hell wanted him to think she still was.

And he was more than willing to go along with it...

"Now I have you where I want you," he growled.

"And what are you going to do with me?"

"Me pirate, you captured maiden?"

She wriggled a little bit, a slow smile stealing across her face. "Maybe captured mermaid instead?"

10

"MY CAPTURED MERMAID?" Andy murmured, his boyish expression melting into a hot look of desire as he glided his hand over her sleek, sudsy curves. "Then I command you to lie there while I please you—"

"But...what about you?"

After all, this was *their* first time, but when his hand passed between her legs, his fingers searching and fondling, thoughts flew zip-zap out of her mind.

"Trust me," he said in that husky, rock-bottom tone. "We'll take *very* good care of me later. But first, now that your toe is miraculously freed..."

In her foggily aroused state, Daphne glanced at her recently liberated foot, lying at the far edge of the tub and wanted to explain to Andy that despite the bizarre reasons for her toe propelling itself into the faucet, there was no miracle about how it got freed. Thanks to his expert use of suds and creams and, oh yes, his big strong hands doing that rubbing-stroking thing, her toe had been saved.

But how in the hell was a woman supposed to carry on a conversation when she was naked, her heartbeat doing a pagan drum solo in her ears, half drugged by a tomcat of a man ready to do simply unthinkable things—she hoped—to her?

So her answer was a breathy, incoherent string of words, most of them the repetition of "suds" and "hands."

"Maybe we shouldn't worry about the toe anymore, hmm?" he said, pressing a finger to her lips. His touch was gentle, damp, tinged with her scent mixed in with almonds and honey and man. Being submerged in deliciously warm water, rubbed by his skilled hands, Daphne Remington had definitely died and gone to sensory-overload heaven.

Andy's blue eyes regarded her assessingly as he slipped his finger from her lips and brushed his other hand along her neck before tunneling his fingers through the hair at her nape.

Anticipation shivered down her spine.

He tightened his hold on her ever so slightly, pulling her forward to meet his lips. She parted hers with a soft moan, waves of heat spiraling through her body as he deepened the kiss, devouring and caressing and nibbling her lips, making love to her mouth with his.

His other hand slid to one breast, then the other, kneading and tugging before his fingers trailed a slow, lazy path down her waist, sloshing the water playfully as he tickled her stomach and made her laugh.

But when his hand grazed lower, excitement mounted between her legs and she writhed a little, anxious and eager. His fingers trailed lower, lower, rubbing slow, lazy circles around her triangle, causing her body to tremble from the sheer, erotic thrill of anticipation.

Then, gently, with the hand still cradling her head, he lifted it a notch, just enough for her to watch what he was doing. The steam in the room had dissipated slightly, making it easier to see, although there was enough of a lingering mist to make it all seem surreal...like a dream.

Through the water, his fingers looked longer, his hands more elegant, as he moved them magically back and forth over her sex. Then he'd stop, skim his fingers down her inner thigh or back up to teasingly tweak a nipple, before he'd return to the spot between her legs.

"I want to see you," he murmured, his breath hot against her ear.

His soft, soapy fingers glided into the tangle of hair again, slipping into the crevice, and gently, very gently, spread her open. Her lower body was but a few inches under the water, the image more a shimmering image than something graphic, which only added to the dreamy eroticism.

"Beautiful," he murmured, stroking his fingers along her cleft. "Where?" he asked huskily.

She shifted her body a little, using her hand to guide him.

Then he touched her *there*.

She moved convulsively against his hand, her breath hard, labored as she succumbed to the sublime ache of his skillful fingers. Sparks flared to life within her, flaming into a wildfire that blazed rampant beneath her skin. She trembled, hearing his dark whispered urgings as though from far away, and she clutched at his neck...panting, greedy for release. She pulled his face to her breasts, moaning out loud as his tongue laved, bit, licked her nipples as his fingers kept massaging, massaging...

The world spun, careened.

Then savage satisfaction tore loose as she plummeted over the edge, the breath exploding from her lungs in a prolonged, low wail as she cried out his name, over and over.

Slowly, slowly, the crescendo subsided and she released a soft sigh of contentment as he gently lowered her head, cradling it like a pillow.

Outside the window, birds twittered as they did every spring, their tremulous song like a counter melody to the gentle rippling of the falls. And Daphne thought how often she'd driven past Maiden Falls on highway I-70, hearing the ice-breaking hush of the falls grow to a raging roar by summer, then chill into slow motion by fall, finally freezing into silence again by winter.

And so went the cycle of life, whether here in Maiden Falls or at home in Denver, the only difference being this man now shared her world. Somewhere over the past few days, she'd let down her walls, let him in and, God forbid, given him the power to break her heart.

Daphne turned her head and gazed deeply into his eyes, loving the drowsy warmth she saw there and wishing she could freeze this moment forever. Like the flash of a photograph, she'd capture this instant so she could always remember how it felt in the aftermath of being made love to by the man of her dreams.

As her heart returned to a normal pace, and she could breathe comfortably again, she searched Andy's face as though seeing him for the first time.

He still had that mischievous air, like a wicked leprechaun, but for the first time she saw lines in his face she'd never noticed before. Deep, furrowed. And she knew he was letting her see his truest self. The Andy who hadn't always had the easiest life, who'd weathered some harsh truths while other kids were still believing in Santa Claus, but that despite it all, or maybe even because of it, he was a better man.

"Ready?" he suddenly asked.

She half nodded, not sure what exactly was in store and not really caring, either. It was their first night as lovers, one they'd always remember, and that's all that mattered.

Andy stood, shook the water off his bare arms although his short-sleeved T-shirt was mostly soaked after their bathtub rendezvous, and grabbed a fat fluffy towel off a rack. He held it wide for her, waiting.

She stood, stepped out of the tub and he wrapped it around her tightly, rubbing her dry, teasing her that she looked like Snow White with that mass of raven hair and porcelain skin, well, except for that smattering of freckles across her button nose...

She laughed, loving every minute of being babied and pampered as though she were the most precious object in this man's world.

Stop, time. Let me have this moment forever.

Andy folded the towel about her, and gave her a friendly pat on her behind, telling her to meet him in the bedroom. Then he stood back and watched the sway of her hips beneath the terry cloth as she waltzed out of the bathroom into the bedroom.

But suddenly the thought of her prancing away, draped in a towel, didn't cut it. An image blasted through his mind—Daphne naked, towel flung aside, and the delicious sight he could see of her in that ceiling-to-floor smoky mirror on the far side of the bed...

His throat suddenly tight, he followed her in two quick strides and ripped away her towel. She gasped, turned, but seeing the look of hot need on his face, her Snow White act suddenly turned dark, sultry...

"I wondered when you'd want me," she whispered.

She drew closer, flattened her palms against his damp T-shirt and stared up at him with such a wanton look, it was all he could do to not take her right there. Rough. Hard.

But he didn't lift a finger.

Instead he said in a husky whisper, "Take off my clothes."

They were standing at the foot of the bed, the overhead chandelier bathing them in a silver-golden glow.

Looking across the room at the mirror, he gazed at her nakedness and marveled at the taut planes of her back. The pert silhouette of her breast. One might call her lean if her sweet waist didn't flare into a pair of nicely rounded hips. And below that was a pair of the longest legs he'd ever seen. The kind that could wrap tightly around a man's neck.

Or waist.

Tonight was going to be one long, hot night...and he planned to experience every deliciously wicked moment of it.

Slowly her fingers inched into the waistband of his jeans and for a moment, they shared a sly this-is-gonna-be-fun smile before suddenly she tugged out the shirt, and he barely had time to raise his arms as she yanked the damn thing over his head and tossed it aside.

He stood there, bare-chested, a bit taken aback.

"Uh, I've heard of fast women before, but can we take this a bit slower?"

"You've *heard* of fast women?" She cocked one fist on her naked hip.

"Okay, I've known a few in my time. But baby, those memories are gone, expunged, because all that matters is you and me and the love we're making tonight. Which—" he popped the first button on his jeans "—we're going to take slower because I want to remember every single moment."

He paused, closed his eyes, secretly hoping he hadn't been a fool. Hoping that what they'd shared these past few days would be more than a few stolen moments.

He opened his eyes and met her gaze. "Sweet lady, I can't read the future, but I do know I'd take these few days with you over a lifetime with anybody else."

Daphne looked momentarily startled. "Andy," she finally said, "You're more than a sweet-talkin' guy. You're a poet."

He didn't want to confess that his reputation as a sweet-talkin' guy hadn't always been a compliment, but more a tagline the guys had given him for his womanizing ways. And when he looked back, he wasn't so proud of that moniker. What did "sweet-talkin'" connote except for the ability to deceive, manipulate?

He wanted to be more than that. He wanted to be a man unafraid to speak the words in his heart.

"Daphne," he whispered, pulling her close. His heart was racing even as, with a feigned casualness, he brushed his mouth across hers before pulling back his head to look down at her.

Say it.

He'd spent years, a damn lifetime, being a guy's guy, never letting down his guard, always being in charge, always being the one to call the shots.

Never saying I love you.

Okay, saying it and *meaning* it.

Because for the first time in his life, Andy Branigan knew how it felt really to be in love, to want to hold and protect and be at a woman's side for the rest of his life. Be willing to tough it out through the bad times because the good times could be so much sweeter and better if shared with someone special. Daphne was his very own renegade, and he'd have her no other way.

"Daphne—"

"Shh," she whispered, cozying closer. She slid her hands, palms down, along his jeans, running her nails up and down his denim-clad thigh muscles, filling him with lazy sensations of pleasure, echoes of the ecstasy they'd shared in the bathtub.

Then her hands wound around his bottom where she pinched him playfully before sweeping back to the front where she cupped his swollen crotch with both her hands and squeezed gently.

"As you were saying?" she whispered.

Like *now* was the time to say it? Maybe he didn't have the suave of, say, a Hugh Grant, but he had enough common sense not to say "I love you" during a serious crotch-clutching moment.

"It can wait," he gasped.

"You sure?" she whispered, moving closer, rubbing her nipples against his bare chest.

If he couldn't do it during a crotch-clutching moment, he sure as hell couldn't during a nipple-rubbing one, either.

"I'm sure, I'm sure," he murmured, barely able to get the words out, the thrill of her pebbled nipples rubbing against his chest flooding him with renewed desire. He leaned his forehead against hers and willingly gave himself up to her caresses, musically chanting her name all the while.

Pop pop.

She undid two more of the buttons on his jeans, then paused, first playing with the springy hair of his crotch before running a finger sensuously around and around the swollen tip of his member peeking out of his unbuttoned pants. He inhaled sharply at the contact, passion pounding hot in his blood.

To hell with slow.

He yanked apart the opening of his pants, popping loose the last two buttons, before tugging them off and kicking them and his briefs aside.

"I want you, Daphne, and I want you bad. *Now.*"

He turned her around so she was facing the mirrors on the far side of the bed, and he watched her reflection, memorizing her, claiming her as he caressed and rubbed her breasts, her hips, her luscious mound. Even from here, he could see her skin's dusty-pink glow, the flush of an aroused woman, and he rubbed his pulsing shaft against her, teasing her, tormenting himself.

"Don't ever let me do anything you don't like," he whispered in her ear, watching her reflection in the mirror.

For a moment, she looked surprised. Then, suddenly she turned slightly and cupped his face with her hands.

"Oh, my dearest," she murmured, her eyes softening with emotion as she pulled down his head and pressed her lips to his, the commitment sealed.

And he found himself, out of the blue, humming the refrain from a love song he once knew, thoughts and emotions crowding his mind and he felt giddy. Stupid happy, like a kid experiencing his first crush, and he suddenly wished he'd remembered to put on music—something sultry and sexy—even while realizing they only needed each other to be "in the mood." Hell, they had the rest of their lives to experiment and play because right now all that mattered was to make love, the first time of many, and that promise had been sealed with her kiss.

He lifted her in his arms, loving the liquid feel of her skin against his, and carried her toward the bed where he gently lowered her onto the satin bedspread. He took a moment to admire her naked beauty, golden in the light from the chandelier, before opening the box and extracting one of the foiled packets.

As he stretched it on his member, he crouched and grazed his lips against her mouth. His tongue flicked the inner pinkness, so soft and wet, before his lips roamed the rest of her body. Lightly over her breasts, over the taut tummy, then sliding down, down until, after kissing her mons, he slid his tongue up her cleft again and again until he felt her body melt.

Then, he stood. Never breaking contact with those sweet eyes dark with arousal, he straddled himself over her and eased his rigid shaft into her secret core, taking his time to slide in slowly, slowly...

He gritted his teeth, fighting his own burning need to lose himself physically, emotionally within her. But when he heard her guttural moan of satisfaction, he gave one last push and filled her completely, fully.

"Daphne...you...feel...so...good." He chanted her name over and over, rocking in tandem with her movements, murmuring words of pleasure while marveling at the dance of emotions across her face. Joy. Smoldering intensity. Vulnerability. When she gathered him tighter into her arms, giving him a look filled with such absolute love and trust, he trembled with the fear of ever losing her.

Then, a look of startled pleasure, a cry of need, and she arched her back as her insides exploded in a series of convulsions. He thrust into her harder, deeper, impaling her one last time before succumbing to his own prolonged, body-shattering release.

And afterward, as they lay in each other's arms, their bodies drenched with sweat, he rolled over and lifted her chin with his finger so their eyes were level and he stared into hers for a long time.

"Daphne," he finally whispered, "I love you."

BELLE LEANED BACK on the love seat, smoking her cigarillo, as she watched Andy and Daphne sleep cradled in each other's arms. Dang if she didn't feel a bit wistful seeing the results of their mutual adoration. Almost made her believe in true love herself.

"Damn I'm good," she muttered before taking another puff.

"Belle, I heard that!"

Belle arched an eyebrow toward the attic at Miss Arlotta. "Well," Belle said, "it's true." Yessiree, Belle's little bag of tricks—lifting the toe into the faucet, the lure of the mirrored bedroom—had been the cherry on the cake, the final acts of turning two total strangers into lovers for life.

Through an exhalation of smoke, Belle stared at the sated lovers, pondering how her worldly life had once been when she sold her body for money. Funny how people sniffed and called it "prostitution" without realizing folks prostituted their own souls every day.

By not following their dreams.

For example, Daphne's soul loved photography and Andy's yearned to write that book on Colorado history. Maybe Belle should plant some thoughts about that, too.

In the morning, Andy still needed to wrap up his article, so Belle would also plant a thought or two about doing one of those "Internet searches" for Jo because it would be Belle's last chance to learn her baby's destiny.

Meanwhile, Belle had a special visit to pay to Miss Arlotta because Belle had a hankerin' to do some negotiating. Like, two—maybe *three*—gold stars for the matchmake of the century?

She floated toward the door, thinking life—or more specifically the afterlife—had never felt so damn good.

"Belle!"

"Sorry, sorry," Belle murmured, rolling her eyes at the attic even while a sly, self-satisfied smile creased her ghostly features.

11

SOMETHING TICKLED Andy's nose. Sleepily, he swiped at it, his fingers getting tangled in rose-scented silky curls.

That woke him up.

He blinked open his eyes and stared at the raven mass of hair, a woman's soft body attached to that lovely head.

Daphne.

He smiled, indulging in the hot, sweet memories of last night's lovemaking. And for a moment, he toyed with a repeat visit. What more perfect way to start the day?

But life wouldn't be so perfect if he didn't finish that damn honeymoon hotel article...and *fast*. He'd promised Frank he'd have the first draft e-mailed to the *Post* last night, and well, toes and faucets and mirrors and...

Well, a lot got in the way.

Andy jumped out of bed, tiptoeing around ripped-open foil packets, empty airplane bottles, piles of candy wrappers and a half-eaten bag of peanuts—oh, right, they'd missed dinner. With no small sense of pride, he counted five condom wrappers.

Several minutes later, he was sitting up in bed, typing like a madman. A few more paragraphs and this baby was done.

"G'morning, sexy," murmured Daphne, looking up at him with a dark lock of hair curling down the middle of her forehead. "You always work in bed?"

"With you, baby, it'll never be work. Unfortunately, my deadline was—" he glanced at the clock on the nightstand. Ten o'clock. Shit. "—fourteen hours ago. Let me wrap up this draft, sweetheart, then I'm all yours."

"I don't mean to bother you," Daphne whispered, suddenly all serious, "but I keep thinking of that baby Jo."

Across the room, the glass decanter rattled.

They both looked at it, back at each other.

"Not the wind," said Daphne.

"Nope, not the wind. Or room service barreling down the hall or any other reason I've concocted in my half-cocked brain these last few days." He squeezed Daphne's hand. "I think that's Belle talking to us and I'm the guy who never believed in ghosts." *Or true love.* A lot had changed this weekend.

The decanter rattled again.

"Holy cow!" Daphne exclaimed, sitting up. "I think she really is talking to us!" Daphne fidgeted with the bed cover "Belle," she announced loudly, "it was you who made both of us dream about being at my ancestor Charlie's kitchen that night, right?"

Rattle rattle.

"Daphne, just talk normally," Andy said quietly. "I think she can hear us fine."

Good thing Andy was accustomed to working on a floor with thirty other reporters all typing and talking at once. Excellent training for staying focused no matter what the hell else was going on...like ghosts who suddenly felt chatty.

Daphne looked pensively at the decanter. "You wanted us to be lovers..."

Rattle.

"But there was something else about being at Charlie's...were we supposed to be Charlie and Sarah?"

Silence.

"The child," Andy whispered, the answer like a smack in the head with a two-by-four. "Hell," he said, staring at the decanter. "Bonnie, or Belle, when you skipped out of Tombstone in 1889 or so, you didn't know you'd been—" He paused, realizing that a woman was a woman even if she was a ghost and he didn't need to blow it by saying something male dumb-ass stupid.

He took a breath, started again. "When you had to flee Tombstone, you weren't aware..."

Lilacs, strong and sweet, suddenly swirled through the room and he had the sense she was agitated, maybe excited, because he was finally hitting on the truth.

"You weren't aware," he repeated gently, "that you were with child." It was something he'd thought before, but had let the thoughts pass. Now it all made sense.

Daphne gasped. "Oh my God! *Jo!* Our baby at the neighboring house was Jo! I guessed it, remember? Well, I didn't know *why*, but I wondered if the child might be named Jo. I wonder if that's why we keep thinking about that little girl. Belle wants to know about her baby."

The decanter rattled so strongly, it skittered slightly across the marble table top.

The long-buried secret brought a surprise mist to Andy's eyes. Him, the guy's guy, getting mushy. Well, hell, it was giving him an answer to his own life. He'd carried rage at his own mother for years, hating her for abandoning him. But suddenly, for the first time in his life, Andy felt empathy for the woman who'd given him birth. She'd had problems, terrible ones, but maybe she'd given him up for his own well-being, and although he'd never know, because she'd long ago passed away, she might have spent her life haunted by the child she'd lost.

A fate not unlike Belle's.

"Bonnie," Andy continued, speaking to the wafting scent, "you gave birth to Jo in 1890?"

Rattle.

"You knew she was nearby, I'd guess, because why else would you pick work in this remote mountain community? There were plenty of top-notch bordellos in Denver."

Rattle.

Then he remembered what the Grand Dame had said. "Yellow fever hit around 1891... You probably thought your baby had died and, oh God, now I realize how you discovered she'd lived."

He turned to Daphne, whose eyes were so wide, only a line of hazel rimmed her black pupils. "Daphne, the night we looked at that old photograph of Charles Remington and the others, remember how the housekeeper and her baby Jo were in the background? That photo was, what, 1893? After all this time, over a hundred years, Belle finally saw that her baby had survived."

The glass decanter rattled, although it seemed quieter, a little sadder. They sat in silence for a long moment, the only sound the almost-rushing babble of the falls.

"If you go downstairs to the historical parlor," Andy said to Daphne, "there's a photo album with a picture of Belle at a picnic. Can't miss her—she's the rowdy one in the back lining up a shot with her revolver." He looked around the room. "Sorry, Belle, but I'm sure being called a rowdy isn't such a big surprise to you." He glanced back at Daphne. "And while you're down there, maybe you'll get one tired, on-deadline writer a cup of that free coffee?"

Daphne jumped out of bed, tossing on her cargo pants and Andy's red fleece jacket. "Coffee, sure thing. Oh my God, Andy, I'll actually see her!" She looked around. "I mean, I know I saw you before, Belle, but now I'll have proof it's really you!"

Daphne shoved on the baseball cap, stuck on her sunglasses and made a mad dash for the door.

"Your shoes," Andy pointed out.

"Right." She slipped into those insane green sky-scrapers and, with a last waggle of her fingers over her shoulder, slammed the door shut behind her.

Andy didn't have the heart to tell her she should've put on a bra. Maybe she thought sunglasses protected her from inquisitive looks, but he seriously doubted anyone would be checking out her eyes.

He looked around the room and smiled, realizing the best story of all had been in this room for years, generations, just waiting for someone to discover it.

A FEW MINUTES later, there was a sharp rap at the door.

Andy, nearly finished with the honeymoon hotel draft, looked up. "Probably forgot her key," he muttered, shoving the laptop aside and hopping out of bed. He grabbed the fluffy towel he'd ripped off Daphne the night before and wound it around his middle as he headed to the door. Not that he wouldn't mind answering the door naked for Daphne, but that didn't mean he wanted to share his stud-boy status with a passing maid or a surprised guest.

He opened the door.

Snap!

He blinked, a dot of white light dancing in front of his eyes. "What the hell—?"

"Where's Daphne Remington?" asked a male voice.

Andy blinked, vaguely recognizing a photographer

and reporter from a rival newspaper. Shit. How'd they know she was here?

He started to speak, ready to do some of the sweet talkin' he was infamous for, when a woman in a corset and lace-trimmed drawers, her hair falling down her back in long auburn waves, strolled between him and the gentleman.

"Looking for someone, boys?" she said in a husky, don't-mess-with-the-lady voice. She jutted out one hip, showing off the pearl-handled revolver wedged in the waistband of her drawers.

Her *drawers*?

With *boots*?

"Da-Daphne?" the photographer rasped.

"Wrong lady," she answered. "Now I'd suggest y'all leave before I call hotel security."

The photographer, a glazed look on his face, raised his camera and started to take another picture.

Belle pulled out her revolver and pointed it in the general below-the-belt vicinity of the two men. "Do that again, and you'll be missing somethin' mighty important to you boys."

The two men speed-walked down the hallway, quickly turning a corner out of view.

Andy, stunned, stared at Belle. No wonder Drake's dying words had been that he loved this woman—she was frickin' incredible. Reminded him of that actress Madeline Stowe, except with auburn hair laced with streaks of copper red. Eyes like a feline, sexy and

green. And that voice...dear God, if the sun didn't
thaw the falls, that whiskey-deep voice could.

He glanced down the hall again just to make sure
the idiots were gone. Then he turned back, murmuring "Thank you."

But Belle was gone, too.

DAPHNE SAUNTERED into the lobby, feeling a bit cocky
after a night of being a wild she-devil in bed, and debated whether to go for the coffee in the lobby first, or
check out the picture of Belle in the historical parlor.

Being Monday morning, few people were around.
No line for coffee, and hell, Daphne was beside herself
with curiosity to verify the woman, well, ghost, she'd
seen was really the notorious gun-toting card shark
Belle Bulette.

She thought back to the sign on Belle's bedroom
door. Never Fold a Good Hand. Wonder if that had
been Belle's guideline for life?

In the historical parlor, a photo album was open
right to a page with a sepia photo of a group of women
in their Sunday finest sitting prettily on blankets, eating chicken and fruit...

And there, in the background was Belle. Couldn't
miss her.

It was the woman Daphne had seen in their room
twice—the day they first walked in, and the time she'd
whispered to Daphne that she and Andy were meant
for each other. Daphne leaned closer and checked out
the familiar tilt of the lady's chin, that to-die-for hair

and get a load of how she stood, ready to square off at some target and shoot at it.

What a woman.

Feeling a bit giddy, as though she'd just met a long-lost friend, Daphne headed back to the lobby for coffee when she spied a copy of the *Denver Post* lying on a table.

Renegade Remington, Runaway Bride?

Her insides turned to ice. She read and reread the heading on the front page, scanning a few of the sentences, her insides roiling with nausea. It was filth, gossip...

And it was written by Andrew Branigan, his name at the top of the article. He'd said he was working on the article just this morning. Like hell. He'd been scamming her all along, writing and sending it in when she wasn't looking, all the while pretending to write some "hotel" story.

She damn near stumbled back through the lobby, dashed madly up the stairs, and threw herself in the room.

"You bastard!"

Andy, leaning over from just unplugging the phone line into the computer, straightened and frowned. "What?"

"You know *exactly* what!" Heat rushed to her face. Her hands shook.

"Uh, no, I don't."

"Liar!" She marched to the phone, punched in a number and waited.

"Mother?" she said, swiping at her eyes. "I want to come home, *now*." Pause. "What?" Daphne dragged the phone as far as the line would go and looked out the bay window. "You're right," she said, her voice breaking. "The media is descending on the inn. I'll ask the concierge for a private room and wait for you. Please hurry. I don't want to stay here one more minute."

Andy, openmouthed, stared as Daphne began throwing items into her purse. Some makeup. Her silk chemise top. She tugged off his pullover.

"Daphne, please, keep it. You need something warm to wear."

She flashed him a screw-you look as she kicked his pullover aside and jammed her arms into her jean jacket, buttoning it with shaking fingers.

She stormed past Andy toward the door, but he caught her arm.

"You don't walk out on me without explaining what the hell's wrong."

She notched her chin higher, her eyes watery with emotion. "Now I know why they call you a sweet-talkin' guy. You sweet talked me with lies. Telling me I could have anonymity—*not*. Promising we'd work on an interview telling *my* side of the Renegade Remington story—*not*. Telling me—" she swallowed hard, barely able to keep her voice level "—telling me you loved me. *Not*."

"Daphne, for God's sake—"

"Read the *Post*, Andy. You got your front-page

story. You'll sell the story elsewhere, too, make big bucks off my reputation, and then you can write that book of your dreams. That's what it's all about, right? What *you get*, not how *you destroy* other people's lives."

"I don't know what you're talking about—"

"Step aside," she said coldly, holding herself ramrod straight, "because I'm walking out of here with the one thing you or any other self-serving asshole can never destroy. *My self-esteem.* At one time, I thought it could be tarnished, walked on. But not anymore. It's mine to nurture and protect...and no matter what *anybody* says or does, it's untouchable."

Holding her head high, she walked out the door.

OVER AN HOUR later, Andy stood in the lobby along with a crowd of guests and hotel staff, staring out the windows at the chaos in front of the inn. Crowding the porch steps was a mass of reporters, mikes, cameras. Standing on the top step was a pale-faced Daphne surrounded by an imposing, bigger-than-life crew of stone-cold profiles making her look like a speck on Mount Rushmore itself. Standing immediately behind her were the Remington clan and their assorted lawyers—or so Andy guessed by their Italian suits, jaded looks, and the number of times they checked their Rolex watches.

And standing next to Daphne, Mr. G. D. McCormick. No, not just standing *next* to, but with his *frickin' arm* around her as though she needed his protection.

Hell, the man hadn't even known she'd run away from *him*, from her life in Denver, the only way she could let down her guard for a few days. Had he ever seen her photographs from the halfway house? Did he have any idea how talented she was?

Or how infectious her laughter was?

Or that she had a way of looking into people's hearts and making them believe in love again? Andy closed his eyes, recalled the scent of her perfume, how it was named for Dulcinea, the woman who moved Quixote to heroic deeds. Who transformed Quixote into a man who believed that without her love, he was like a tree without leaves, or a body without a soul.

That's how Andy felt. Bereft, empty.

He'd lost his Dulcinea.

He looked out the window again.

Someone had brought her a new set of clothes. Daphne looked ridiculously demure in a pink suit— knee-length for God's sake—with matching pink, and *very* proper, pumps. Worse was her hair. The raven mass had all the curl taken out of it and was sleeked back in some kind of bun that even a nun would scoff at.

"Nothing significant happened here," she answered some reporter, her voice like a ghost of the Daphne he knew, "except I needed a little R&R."

G. D. McCormick pulled her closer to his side and leaned toward the microphone, "On behalf of my fiancée—"

Fiancée?

"I chastise the press for their sloppy reporting and sensationalist intent. In the future, stick to issues critical to Colorado's future—tourism, reemployment assistance, promotion of Colorado's agricultural products..."

Yada yada.

Of course, old "Gordo" would find an opportunity to bang his political drum. Did he even care that Daphne felt betrayed and traumatized? No, it was a promo op for G. D. McCormick. Andy could march out there right now, take Daphne by the hand and run to his Jeep, the hero saving the damsel on his mighty steed, but he'd already made a big enough mess of things.

Not that he'd known the story would break the way it did, or even that he could have stopped it, but, out of respect for Daphne, he wouldn't create more public chaos and pain in her life.

Anyway, he'd tried to explain after he'd discovered what happened, but hotel security denied him admission to her room. Daphne Remington, he'd been told in no uncertain terms, refused to see him.

Andy turned away from the media circus, weaved his way through the crowd in the lobby, headed back up the stairs to their room.

My room. Not ours.

Earlier, after Daphne had called him a liar and told him to read the front page of the *Post*, he'd done just that. He'd been more surprised than anyone to see the horrific heading—Renegade Remington, Runaway

Bride? Sick to his stomach, he'd skimmed the story. Half the words were his from the interview, but skewered and pulled out of context to give the story a seamy slant. Worse, his name had headed the article as though he'd written it.

To Daphne, he looked like the biggest lying jerk who'd ever walked the planet.

He'd immediately called Frank, who'd explained all hell had broken loose at the *Post* when they got word a rival paper was ready to print a hot story about a certain *Post* reporter shacking up with the infamous, and very engaged to a possible future governor, Daphne Remington. Frank's boss demanded to see *all* of the stories Andy was currently writing, which was how the interview was yanked off the server, and the publisher himself gave the go-ahead to wipe out the almost-ready-to-print heading and story and replace it with the Renegade Remington one.

Another writer had done a fast-and-dirty revision and it had gone to press.

Frank had apologized profusely. The *Post*'s circulation needed a boost, the powers-that-be wanted to beat the competition...the rest of Frank's words had been a blur...

Andy opened the minibar and pulled out an airplane bottle. But when he smelled the sting of whiskey, memories of that night when they'd first kissed came flooding back. How she'd stuck her pinkie in the bottle, "begged" him to kiss her, how he'd nearly lost his mind tasting her lips for the very first time...

I gotta get out of this freaking room.

Too many memories. Too much heartache.

He had halfheartedly tossed some things into his backpack when he looked up and caught his reflection in the smoky mirror on the back wall.

Next to him stood Belle.

"I'm sorry," she whispered.

He nodded. "Me, too." He swallowed back the rock in his throat, then whispered, "I'll keep looking for Jo. I promise."

He swore he saw the glimmer of a tear in her eye as she faded into nothingness.

THE JUDGE and Miss Arlotta sat behind the table, staring at Belle. The judge's normally twinkling blue eyes were somber; Miss Arlotta's red lips were tight. Belle noticed a copy of the *Post*, with that damn headline, lying on the table between them.

"Miss Arlotta and I have reached a unanimous decision," the judge said solemnly, his bushy mustache quivering as he spoke, "that you be stripped of all earned notches."

All? "What about the three gold bonus stars?"

"*Including* the three gold bonus stars you negotiated with Miss Arlotta at candle-lighting yesterday."

The judge still used terms from their real-life days. Like candle-lighting for nighttime, and Belle's heart twinged recalling how joyous Andy and Daphne had been when they'd fallen asleep last night in each other's arms.

"But surely the three gold stars must mean I can keep *something.* One notch, maybe two?"

Miss Arlotta shook her head of pale-blond curls. "Belle, darlin', this isn't a negotiation." She waggled her fingers and the scroll with the golden rules appeared in her hands, which she quickly scanned. "You not only broke at least four of the rules, but you committed the greatest grievance of all—you broke two hearts."

Miss Arlotta paused, releasing the scroll, which fluttered into thin air. "What the judge and I also decided," she said, her voice strained, "is that for the nine bedpost notches you earned, you've now earned as many black marks."

Nine black marks? It would take Belle years, lifetimes, to even get back to square one!

"But I'm innocent!" She paced back and forth. "The *Denver Post* made the decision to run that story—"

"Those reporters you threatened," cut in Miss Arlotta, darting a look at the revolver in Belle's waistband, "would have left with zero evidence if only *Andy* had answered the door. But, no, they got an eyeful of a—" she tapped the paper "—'scantily clad bodyguard' who 'threatened them with a gun' so they questioned other guests, got an eyewitness report from some woman who accused Daphne of lascivious behavior the previous morning at the complementary coffee urn. One thing led to another and the *Post* lifted that sordid story, *and* theirs to press...a story they *never* would've run if a certain ghost hadn't materialized in the wrong place at the wrong time."

Belle stared out the window at the blue sky and realized it was going to be a long, long time—another hundred, two hundred years?—before she'd ever leave this hotel.

Her only hope being that maybe, before his soul departed for the great beyond, Andy Branigan might discover what had happened to Jo. That thought alone would be her solace for many, many years to come.

12

"DAPHNE, darling, what happened to your hair?"

Daphne's mother, sipping her morning Earl Grey, stared at Daphne's head. Next to her at the breakfast table was Daphne's father, eating toast while reading the paper. Her sister Iris was studying her manicured nails and Gordo, as usual, was answering his always-ringing cell phone.

"Gordon here." He frowned, listening. "Then we'll paper them with discovery..."

He'd been showing up every single morning these past three weeks, ever since the Maiden Falls debacle, determined to woo Daphne back to engagement status. There'd been dinners, a night at the theatre and talks—or, as Gordo called them, negotiations.

But through it all, she'd refused to put the ring back on.

As with most disagreeable things, the rest of the family simply pretended not to notice, but they sure as hell had ol' Gordo there night and day, as though his permanent presence would change Daphne's mind. But she'd been doing a lot of thinking these past three weeks as well as meeting with her personal lawyer. As to the former, she'd decided why great-great-great-

great-granddad Charles hadn't been as happy after striking it rich. All those millions cost him his truest self, buying more headaches than happiness. Which reaffirmed that she didn't want to live the rest of her life pretending to be someone she wasn't.

As for the latter, well, it'd taken these past few weeks for her lawyer to research the fine print of her trust, and also unearth some enlightening facts about the recent *Post* article.

"My hair," she answered her mother, "is back to its natural state. Curly. Just like my life is going back to its natural state."

Her mother looked up. Her father lowered his paper. Iris stopped her manicure inspection. Gordo hung up his cell.

Daphne rolled back her shoulders. "I was just advised that there have been some things going on underneath the table that have been kept secret from me."

Gordo frowned.

"Andy," Daphne continued, "is not personally responsible for the *Post* publishing libel. And he can't be sued individually because he didn't put the spin on that story, either. That means, in plain English, Andy Branigan didn't say or do anything wrong. The evidence is clear that he never meant that story for publication. In fact, he tried to protect me. In fact..."

She swore she could hear Belle whispering again, "You and that man are meant for each other." God,

Daphne just hoped Andy still felt that way. Hoped it wasn't too late.

"Andy loves me. And I love him."

She paused, pulled the ring out of her pocket and set it in front of Gordo. He stared at it, his face ashen.

"You're a good lawyer, Gordo. You taught me something very important. No consideration, no contract. Our deal is closed."

She smiled, feeling better than she had in weeks. Three, to be exact. "That's all," she said. "I'd stay for breakfast, but I have a life to catch up on." *And a man to sweet-talk, if he'll let me.*

She walked away, ready to be Renegade Remington again.

ANDY TOSSED the foam basketball into the plastic hoop on the wall between his and another reporter's cubicle. It helped him think to play foam basketball, which he'd been doing a lot over the past three weeks, ever since the fiasco at the Inn at Maiden Falls. He was back at the *Post*, finishing yet another fluff piece on zoning violations in metro Denver. But on the side he'd been researching Jo Sutherland, which had become a fascinating journey because not only had he discovered the whereabouts of the long-lost diamond-dust mirror, the "Lady of the Lake," he was also on the verge of finding the last in a string of Belle's living descendants.

His boss Frank, damn near groveling to make amends after the Renegade Remington story, had promised to run the "Lady of the Lake" story in the *Post*, and Andy was mulling over how great it'd be as one of the stories in his Colorado history book...when and if he ever got around to writing it.

Phoomf.

Andy bounced the foam ball off the wall, missing the hoop.

With all the nonstop jabbering on this floor, it was almost impossible to hear oneself think, much less hear the *phoomf* of a foam ball hitting a wall. What was with the sudden quiet?

He looked behind him.

There stood Daphne.

His heart wrenched as he looked into those hazel eyes, remembering how they sparkled when she laughed or turned soft when they'd made love. She was dressed down, jeans and work shirt. Her hair back to that curly mass that didn't seem to know which way was up.

Hardly the Daphne he'd last seen at the inn, dressed in that insane pink number, responding numbly to reporters' questions. No, the woman who stood before him now was *his* Daphne, the wild-at-heart girl he'd fallen in love with three weeks ago.

But appearances, as any jaded reporter knew, could be deceiving.

Besides, what was really important at this very moment was for him to clear the air finally. Face to face. Explain how the publisher himself gave the go-ahead on that damn interview, how another writer rewrote Andy's words, how he'd never meant to hurt her....

How Andy Branigan was a different man these days.

Around the office, his buddies ribbed him that he'd gone from sweet-talkin' to no-talkin'. Maybe that's because he spent a lot of time pondering if a man's regrets stayed with him from this life into the next.

"Please, sit," he said, his voice low, raspy, like someone he'd never heard before. Well, hell, just being *near* her was disturbing enough without trying to *talk*.

"Thanks," she said, and he swore she looked almost grateful. What? That he'd offered her a seat?

He looked around. Like there were any available. Desks, chairs, even the floor were littered with everything from books to gym bags. Some joker had even dragged in a Stop sign. Newsrooms were worse than dorm rooms.

Andy stood. "Here," he said, offering her his chair.

"No, really..."

"I insist."

She did, setting down her camera case and he noticed her hand. No ring.

"Out taking pictures?" He gestured toward the case. *No ring?*

"May's perfect for driving into the Rockies, maybe stopping at Georgetown or Leadville, taking some photographs. Thought you might like to join me?" A blush raced to her cheeks and he realized that despite

their external niceties, she was about as uncool inside
as he was.

"I jumped ahead," she said, looking apologetic.

"Sorta." Like about a mile.

"I thought you'd betrayed me," she blurted. When
he started to speak, she held up her hand, which he
noticed was shaking. Daphne, *nervous*? Why? But before he could ask, she continued.

"I was just advised this morning by my attorney
that the interview was not only *downloaded* without
your knowing, but that another writer revised it."

More like mucked it over, big time. "That's correct," he
said quietly.

"And you could have reprinted the original interview at any point during the last few weeks, made a
lot of money, but you didn't."

"Protecting you was more important than some
damn check."

Her smile was so sweet, so—dare he think it?—loving, damn if he wasn't having trouble breathing.

"So, I was thinking," she said softly, although Andy
knew every reporter in a ten-foot radius was straining
to hear every single word. "Let's go for a ride. I'll take
photographs of the places you want to write about.
Let's start your book on Colorado history."

"Together—for only *that*?" Okay, just because he'd
gone from sweet-talkin' to no-talkin' didn't mean he'd
lost the talent for opening mouth wide and inserting
both feet.

With a shy grin, she waggled her fingers. "I'm not engaged."

One of the guys in the back of the room whistled, another yelled, "Go for it, Branigan!"

He made a mental note to strangle them later. Barehanded.

But right now, he had to know something.

He crouched down next to her chair and drew close to her ear. "Thought you were up for a hefty trust fund if you married Mr. McCormick," he whispered.

She shifted her head, gave him a look, then leaned forward, her lips nearly touching his. "I've requested half of it be given to Mrs. Allen's Halfway House," she whispered, her breath warm and sweet against his lips. "The other half is still held in trust." She winked. "I have a good lawyer."

Then she kissed him. No, not just a kiss. She seared his lips with hers, jolting him with enough voltage to char the whole damn planet, carrying on as though it was just the two of them, alone.

Hardly alone.

In the background, Andy heard the typing of reporters' fingers wanting to be the first to turn in the story of Renegade Remington and her Sweet-Kissin' Man.

Epilogue

BELLE FLOATED PAST her room, smiling at the Do Not Disturb sign on her door. Inside were Mr. and Mrs. Andrew Branigan, newlyweds after a June wedding, and based on the sounds from within they sure as hell didn't need any more wedded-bliss tips from Belle!

"Belle, I heard that!"

"Was hoping you did, Miss Arlotta," muttered Belle, floating upward toward the attic after being summoned by the judge himself.

Moments later, Belle stood in front of the "antique" dining-room table, one of the stored pieces of furniture used whenever a jury was called to session in the attic. Behind the table sat twelve of Belle's peers, everyone from Sunshine to the Countess to Rosebud. Smack in the middle sat Flo, her shawl as tightly wrapped as her pursed lips.

The judge cleared his throat. "Today we're here," he said, sitting in his armchair next to the table, "to pass judgment on Belle Bulette and to determine whether she can ascend to the jurisdiction of the highest court—"

"The Big Picnic in the Sky," corrected Miss Arlotta, standing behind him, her arms crossed over her ample bosom.

He nodded, then continued solemnly, "I hold in my hand—" he held up a piece of paper "—a verdict form indicating the jury has unanimously concluded that all black marks are expunged and the former nine bedpost notches reinstalled, *including* the reinstatement of three recently negotiated gold marks, because of the overwhelming character of the passion that Miss Belle Bulette cooked up between a Mr. Andy Branigan and a Miss Daphne Remington, two heretofore unknown lovers who are, even as I speak, setting new indoor records at the Inn at Maiden Falls."

Miss Arlotta placed her hand on the judge's shoulder and gave it a squeeze.

Sunshine smiled slyly at Belle, while Rosebud surreptitiously tapped her fingers on a newspaper in front of her, which struck Belle as odd since Rosebud normally carted a book everywhere.

The judge stood, adjusted his waistcoat. "Now the judgment and sentence of this court are that you be taken, with all due and deliberate speed, to ascend to the appropriate heights—"

"Big Picnic," quietly corrected Miss Arlotta.

"—and assume your position in heaven for a job miraculously done."

Through the ceiling, a golden staircase suddenly appeared.

"Have you any final words?" asked Miss Arlotta, her eyes bright with emotion.

Belle paused, looked at the girls, still a bit amazed Flo had voted on her behalf, then said, "Yes. I regret I never told my dearest Drake that I loved him." She swallowed, hard. "That I still love him."

Down the staircase descended a male form, tall and dashing, finally stopping on the bottom step.

Drake.

"I could never come to you completely, darlin' girl," he said in that deep, rich voice that filled the room, "until you believed in true love." He extended his hand. "As you always said, Bonnie, never fold a good hand."

She'd taken a step toward the stairs when Rosebud, sitting at the end of the table nearest the stairs, cleared her throat. "Ahem!"

Belle looked at the news story that Rosebud was pointing to. Written by Andrew Branigan with the heading "Lady of the Lake, Wedding Gift to Remington's Housekeeper in 1895, Reunited with Jo Sutherland's Great-great-great-granddaughter."

"Drake, look." Belle exclaimed, her heart aching with love for him and pride at their greatest achievement—having created life. All the years of secret heartbreak were wiped out as she realized hers and Drake's blood still lived on.

Still, they'd missed out on so much.

She took his hand. Together, they began ascending the steps.

"We may have missed things on earth, darlin' girl," he said, answering her thoughts, "but we have eternity to catch up. First in line is our daughter Jo, who can't wait to get to know her mama..."

Belle held tightly on to Drake's hand, staring up at the golden light, so bright, nearly blinding, so much ahead.

Her soul was finally free.

* * * * *

The ghosts aren't finished yet!
Look for CAN'T BUY ME LOVE
Temptation 981 by Heather MacAllister
the next book in THE SPIRITS ARE WILLING
series. On sale July 2004 at your favorite retailer.

New York Times bestselling author

VICKI LEWIS THOMPSON

celebrates Temptation's 20th anniversary— and her own—in:

#980

OLD ENOUGH TO KNOW BETTER

When twenty-year-old PR exec Kasey Braddock accepts her co-workers' dare to hit on the gorgeous new landscaper, she's excited. Finally, here's her chance to prove to her friends—and herself—that she's woman enough to entice a man and leave him drooling. After all, she's old enough to know what she wants—and she wants Sam Ashton. Luckily, he's not complaining….

Available in June wherever Harlequin books are sold.

HARLEQUIN® *Blaze*™
HARLEQUIN® *Temptation*®

Single in South Beach

Nightlife on the Strip just got a little hotter!

Join author Joanne Rock as she takes you back to
Miami Beach and its hottest singles' playground.
Club Paradise has staked its claim in the decadent
South Beach nightlife and the women in charge are
determined to keep the sexy resort on top. So what will
they do with the hot men who show up at the club?

GIRL GONE WILD
Harlequin Blaze #135
May 2004

DATE WITH A DIVA
Harlequin Blaze #139
June 2004

HER FINAL FLING
Harlequin Temptation #983
July 2004

Don't miss the continuation of this red-hot series from Joanne Rock!
Look for these books at your favorite retail outlet.

If you enjoyed what you just read,
then we've got an offer you can't resist!

Take 2 bestselling
love stories FREE!

Plus get a FREE surprise gift!

eHARLEQUIN.com

For **FREE online reading,** visit
www.eHarlequin.com now and enjoy:

Online Reads
Read **Daily** and **Weekly** chapters from
our Internet-exclusive stories by your
favorite authors

Red-Hot Reads
Turn up the heat with one of our more
sensual online stories!

Interactive Novels
Cast your vote to help decide how these
stories unfold...then stay tuned!

Quick Reads
For shorter romantic reads, try our
collection of Poems, Toasts, & More!

Online Read Library
Miss one of our online reads?
Come here to catch up!

Reading Groups
Discuss, share and rave with other
community members!

For great reading online,
visit www.eHarlequin.com today!

HARLEQUIN®

Temptation

When the spirits are willing...
Anything can happen!

Welcome to the Inn at Maiden Falls, Colorado. Once a
brothel in the 1800s, the inn is now a successful honeymoon
resort. Only, little does anybody guess that all that marital
bliss comes with a little supernatural persuasion....

Don't miss this fantastic new miniseries. Watch for:

#977 SWEET TALKIN' GUY by Colleen Collins
June 2004

#981 CAN'T BUY ME LOVE by Heather MacAllister
July 2004

#985 IT'S IN HIS KISS by Julie Kistler
August 2004

THE SPIRITS
ARE WILLING

Available wherever Harlequin books are sold.

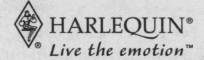

HARLEQUIN®
Live the emotion™

www.eHarlequin.com